KEEP

Ruthless Billionaires

Aarti V Raman

Copyright © Aarti V Raman 2022

All Rights Reserved.

ISBN 979-8-88629-377-7

ALSO BY AARTI V RAMAN

THE MILLIONAIRE FOE$

In Love With Her Millionaire Foe

In Debt To Her Millionaire Foe

Engaged To Her Millionaire Foe

In Bed With Her Millionaire Foe

Seducing Her Millionaire Foe

Deceived By Her Millionaire Foe

Betraying Her Millionaire Foe

Inherited By Her Millionaire Foe

A Millionaire Foes' Reunion

The Millionaire Foes Boxset (1-4)

The Millionaire Foes Boxset (5-8)

RUTHLE$$ BILLIONAIRE$

Claim

Keep

Burn

HER MERCENARY PROTECTOR

To Love Honor and Avenge

To Love Honor and Betray

FILTHY RICH GEEK$

Her Millionaire's Secret

Her Millionaire's Salvation

A Tale of Two Christmases

Her Millionaire's Secret

Her Millionaire's Redemption

A Filthy Rich Geek's Wedding

The Filthy Rich Geeks Boxset Collection

THOSE DANGEROUS ROYALS

Renegade

Chaos

A Night Out With Royals

STANDALONES

The Worst Daughter Ever

With You I Dance

Days Of Our Lives

Marrying Her Millionaire Foe

Something Old, Something New (Out of circulation)

DEDICATION

This book is dedicated to

Mom, my own True North.

Becca Syme who saved my career and my brain and my very life. You are a rockstar, Becca! THANK YOU.

The one and only, the inimitable Jackson Maine aka Bradley Charles Cooper. Drake has been you since I wrote one line about you in a book called Second Chance ten years ago.

A Devilish Lucifer for the crazy eyes.

Nashit and Beth, for being friends trusted and true.

My Kunju, my PM, Pudding's Amma who made the writing of this book possible on the fifth of June, 2021.

And the Big Guy in the Sky.

DRAKE & ANYA'S SOUNDTRACK

- Every Breath You Take (feat. Tom Ellis & Debbie Gibson) By Lucifer cast, Tom Ellis, Debbie Gibson
- Devil Devil By MILCK
- In the Air Tonight By Jon Howard
- Flood By Lhotse, Ellem
- Shallow By Lady Gaga, Bradley Cooper
- Can You Hear Me By UNSECRET, Young Summer
- Creep (feat. Tom Ellis) By Lucifer Cast, Tom Ellis
- Minefields By Faouzia, John Legend
- Valkyrie By Battle Tapes
- Kids By Robbie Williams, Kylie Minogue
- Let's Go Out Tonight By The Blue Nile
- My Love Will Never Die By AG, Claire Wyndham
- Hallelujah By FVR DRMS
- I Found By Amber Run
- Not Your Hero By Becky Shaheen, Mally

ONE

"For a new bride, you look like shit, sis," Ishqi said bluntly as she wandered a shady pawn shop off Orchard Street, that weekend. She took a deep drag of the vape pen she carried. "God, I missed this. Are you done, Anya?"

Anya pocketed the hefty roll of dollars the pawn broker handed her. "Thank you, *ah-ma*." She told the kindly, white-haired matron minding the store. "I'm so glad you liked my pieces."

"This sapphire alone is worth ten times what I gave you, lah. Are you sure you don't mind waiting a few days?" Mama Jong asked Anya again, as she had thrice before. "My son says he'll contact the bank tomorrow and get you more funds."

Anya shook her head, so violently she almost gave herself whiplash. "No. I need the money now. Thank you so much for your kindness, Mama Jong. And you." She gave her sister a sharp look. "The sign clearly says No Smoking, Ishqi."

Ishqi waved her vape pen around, leaving a trailer of hot cinnamon vapor. "I'm not."

She looked like an angry fairy in her rainbow shorts and Doc Martens over fishnet stockings with a baby tee shirt and purple suspenders. The first thing she'd done once she'd been let out of jail yesterday was use Swati's emergency credit card and get herself spa'd up.

Her pixie-cut hair was now a curling purple mess, while an inch thick coal black mascara coated her fake lashes.

"Are you crying, Anya?" Ishqi asked curiously.

Anya shook her head, as the wet haze passed. As quickly as it had come. It came without warning over the last few days. Threatening to swallow her whole where she stood sometimes. And, each time, it was more difficult to wrest her control back so she wouldn't.

It came without warning ever since…

"No," Anya answered quietly. "I'm not a new anything, Ishqi, so stop saying that, will you?"

Ishqi shrugged. "Fine by me. I was just making polite conversation. I won't bring it up again."

They exited the dingy store full of collectibles and curios and emerged into a side street. It was almost afternoon, so the restaurants and pubs on the other side of the street were full of patrons.

Life was buzzing as it usually did on the weekends.

Ishqi bounced on the balls of her feet. "Can we grab something to eat, Anya? I don't want to make mom cook something specifically, since you're not coming back with me. I'm starving for some real *nasi goreng lemak*." She even added an urchin-like smile which melted Anya's heart.

Usually.

But now the idea of spooning in the spicy ramen noodle soup was enough to churn Anya's stomach. "Can we get it to go?" She smiled back. "I have some work to wrap up and I was hoping to get a jump start on next sem's course reading."

"I guess that's fine."

Ishqi dashed across the street, her ironic Hello Kitty backpack bouncing on her pert back.

Anya caught a sight of her own reflection in one of the restaurant glass walls. She looked like a ghost – in her all black tee and jeans outfit. Her hair severely pulled back in a braid, not a speck of makeup on her face. In fact, nothing on her face.

No animation. No color at all.

He'd actually drained her of color. That bastard.

Anya hurried and followed Ishqi into the restaurant. Because she had come very close to breaking her silent promise to herself.

She would not think of Drake Fallahil anymore. Not for a second.

He did not deserve it.

He deserved less than nothing from her, actually. Least of all the gift she'd given him without bothering to weigh the consequences.

It was the reason she'd pawned every single piece of jewelry he'd ever given her, the wedding ring, the sapphire necklace, and his expensive phone, just two weeks ago, with no compunction.

The money had been used to pay for the lawyer's retainer for Ishqi, resulting in her case being expedited and she'd actually been let out early for good behavior, pending further investigation.

She'd have given the clothes away too but she didn't want some other poor unfortunate woman to wear them and experience the same nightmare she was living. So she'd packed them into a trash bag and left it in the trash chute of the penthouse the second she'd cabbed back from the disastrous scene at his office.

She'd have moved out of his very orbit but she'd signed her name on the dotted line and pride demanded she stay put.

Besides, the fucking bastard hadn't bothered to as much as text her after she'd fled his office. He could be in Outer Mongolia for all she cared now.

Ishqi shook Anya's shoulders. So hard that her teeth rattled. She looked annoyed. "You want bubble tea to go with your *lemak*?"

Anya shook her head. "No, thanks, honey. I'm not hungry. You get whatever you want."

Ishqi held a palm out.

Anya stared at her. "What?"

"We have to pay for the food, don't we? I forgot to get mom's card and I'm not adding this to my payment app." She smiled sweetly. "This is your treat."

Anya handed over a few bills to Ishqi and exited the restaurant. It was beginning to make her feel like the walls were caving in. She leaned against one of the graffiti-ed walls and gulped in deep breaths.

~ ~ ~ ~ ~ ~

The expression on Ishqi's face right now was the same as Drake's had been. As her mom always had.

This ridiculous hope that Anya would make everything better. She'd fix everything by breaking herself into two. Because they were *special* and she wasn't, so her only job was to accommodate them.

Her mom had depended so heavily on her till the operation and discarded her when she'd learned to stand on her own two feet. Ishqi was always self-centered, almost to the point of oblivion. Only, now Anya could see it so clearly. It was appalling.

Her sister only cared about herself. She'd not even bothered to thank Anya for the food or the fact that she'd paid for the lawyer's fees with jewelry she'd been given by her husband. She *expected* Anya to clean up her mess.

And *her fucking husband* was the worst of all. The worst offender.

He'd known the truth. He'd kept it from her. He'd not lied to her but what he'd done was worse.

Drake had used her.

Over and over.

And, the sorriest part was, for one second when he'd looked stricken… when he'd wanted to explain the truth to her, she wanted to listen to him. She'd *wanted* him to be different. Someone who cared about her, first.

But he wasn't.

Anya wasn't special. He'd wanted her to accommodate his special life at the cost of her own pride and self-worth.

And she was *damned* if she'd do it for him. No matter how he made her feel. No matter how she felt every time she *moved,* as if she could still feel him – thick and hard and perfect – inside her. Feeding her damned soul with his power. With him.

She hated herself most of all because she'd trusted this man to be safe. To be different. When he'd shown her, over and over again, that he was the literal devil incarnate.

Selfish. Depraved. Unconscionable.

~ ~ ~ ~ ~

Her phone, her old phone, buzzed. She answered without bothering to see the caller. "Yes, hello?"

"Anya?" Mili Iyer's sympathetic tones floated through the call. "Are you crying?"

"No. What?" She gritted out.

Anya touched a hand to her cheek. It came away sopping wet. She discovered she'd slouched almost to the ground with the force of her tears. Her epiphanies.

"Oh my god." She looked at her glistening hand. "I am crying."

Mili cursed stridently. "I am going to kill Drake when I see him. If ever."

Anya flinched. "I don't want to hear his name," she bit out. "Ever. Again."

"I know, love. I'm so sorry." Mili sounded so sympathetic, pitying even.

Anya wanted to scream at her to stop. But none of this was Mili's fault. She'd told Anya the truth about Drake the second they'd met.

He always got his way.

And look where not remembering it had gotten Anya.

"It's okay." She wiped her streaming face briskly. "What's up, Mili? Is there a problem with the projections I created for the new fund?"

"No," Mili answered slowly. "The Verdant Fund set up is done so perfectly, Anya. You have a real knack for cutting through the bullshit and explaining the logic behind the money. It's unlike anything I've ever seen. And I hate doing these decks so, thank you twice over."

The project was a hypothetical set up for structuring a Green Fund, where the investors and promoters were committed to using the money to mitigating climate change through alternative resources. Rerouting projects such as space exploration, tech innovation, mass production to something that would not kill the remaining forty percent of rainforests.

In fact, over the course of working on the project, Anya had become privy to the many ways, big and small, Fallahil Inc. supported and championed causes decidedly anti-capitalist in nature.

Drake had bought mammoth tracts of forest land in Asia, especially South East and South, and South America, and was reforesting it, acre by acre. His companies paid women equal wage, sexual harassment cells trickled down to the ground level, with legal action being levied immediately if ever someone was found abusing their power.

Not to mention what he'd done for the freaking Rhinoceres Project, single-handedly pouring millions into it to procure the necessary permits to mate the last remaining rhinoceros with a female.

She'd actually stumbled across a memo that Drake had written about the core seven hundred startups he'd invested in, where female hiring was at an all-time high and how the lack of a turnover had resulted in increased profits. It was a feminist manifesto couched in economic value.

She'd hardened her bruised heart each time she'd read about yet another silent contribution the man had made to further the cause of an ism, by remembering what he'd told her.

All of it was for profit, for business.

It had worked. Or, so she liked to think.

Anya smiled. "Working on this set up saved my sanity, so I have to thank you, Mili. But if that's not why you're calling, what's up?"

Mili was quiet for a long moment. "Drake called me from Australia where he's been in meetings for the last two weeks, you know."

"So?" Anya was cold, queenly. "What's it got to do with me?"

She didn't care about him anymore, not that she ever had. Beyond interning at his vastly interesting company.

She did not absolutely care that the fucking *cowardly* bastard had fled the country the same night she'd left the penthouse and stayed away in a poor imitation of a decent person. She wished he'd done that the first night they'd met.

"Well, he wants…Can I just read the message he sent me so you don't hate me for being in the middle of this?"

"Don't worry, Mili. I already know he's responsible for the mountains rising and the seas boiling," Anya reassured her. "I am not going to shoot the messenger. Although, I have to wonder. Why does someone who has a Harvard MBA and a Yale Law degree work for this despicable jerk?"

"Because," Mili sighed. "Very occasionally, almost without wanting to, he saves the damn world from burning down."

And other times he wrecks it.

Anya kept her harsh words to herself. "Read the message," she instructed. "Let's get this over with."

"Sending a charter jet for you for Saturday night. Have to attend AllMart CEO's wedding to the MD. Attendance is mandatory. – Drake."

Anya blinked. "What…what is happening?" She knew of AllMart. Any B-school student knew of the chain of departmental stores across Midwest US, headquartered in Chicago and helmed by Zara Subramanian, one of the youngest CEOs ever.

Mili sighed, loud and clear. "Drake's sister's sister-in-law is getting married. You both are invited to the wedding. It's in Chicago. And, attendance…"

"Is mandatory."

"Anya, I'm so *sorry.*" Mili was distressed.

But Anya wasn't. She was filled with cold, righteous purpose. The melancholy and endless grief eating away at her was receding slowly under this new clarity. She didn't think about the instant of poisonous ache under her heart when she heard the word's *Drake's sister*.

The man had an actual family, instead of coming out as the devil spawn she knew him to be.

She focused instead on the fact pertaining to her.

Drake had done something she didn't expect him to do. Something she'd thought not possible.

Something that gave her freedom to do what she had to. Make him pay a thousand times over for the way he'd treated her.

Drake had broken his word and reneged on his deal. He'd not left her alone.

Now, she could do the same.

She was going to go be the world's worst bride at this wedding that was important to Drake and make him pay.

"Mili," Anya murmured. "Can you take the rest of the afternoon off? I need help with my bridal trousseau."

Mili whooped. "Fuck yeah, sister. I'll do you one better. I'll bring the Black Amex Drake keeps locked up in the safe for special emergencies. Orchard Street had better watch out."

"Yes," Anya vowed. "Everyone had better watch out. Here comes the bride…"

TWO

Until, Drake actually saw Anya emerge from the Gulfstream he'd sent for her on Friday night, he did not believe that she'd actually come to Chicago.

He'd been in the middle of negotiating an Australia co-promoter for The Verdant Fund project – being simultaneously set up in seventeen countries - when Dev, Zara's Dev video-called him up personally and invited him to come to their wedding.

"It would mean a lot to Zara and Lily and to me, Drake. So I hope you make it," Dev told him without prevarication.

"I thought you guys were planning a Diwali shindig. Wasn't that the plan?"

"It was," Dev had agreed cheerfully. "Plans change. Don't they?" He'd looked rested, relaxed…a man in his element in the shorts and tee shirt he'd worn while lounging under a sycamore tree at Sycamore Drive.

"Yeah," Drake had murmured. "That they do."

He thought about his own plan – never to marry, never to attach himself to anyone. All blown to smithereens because of his damnable need to control everything and everyone who tried to manipulate him.

"Besides, a summer wedding is perfect for the weather here." Dev grinned. "And we miss seeing your handsome face, you know."

Drake made some random comment to that. Envying this man he could buy and sell five times over with his accumulated net worth. At one point, he'd even wanted to when he'd thought he wanted Zara, the CEO of AllMart, and Dev's fiancée.

But Zara had only ever had eyes for Dev, the love of her young, golden life. And Drake wasn't cruel enough to tear them apart for his own selfish gains.

Not like he had with…he shut the thought down cold.

"So, you'll come, right?"

Drake wanted to refuse. Of course, he did. He did not want to socialize with anyone. Particularly the overly familial Subramanians, who made it all look so easy.

"Sure. Of course, I will. It'll be great seeing everyone again."

"Thanks, man. I'll inform the wedding planner people you're coming. Plus one?" Dev checked something off his phone.

Drake almost shook his head. "Yes," he said instead. "I'll be bringing someone."

Dev wisely did not pry more and they'd finished the conversation with Dev shooting the relevant details to Drake.

~ ~ ~ ~ ~

Before he could second guess himself, Drake immediately sent Mili a missive informing her of the change in his travel plans and included a terse note for *her.*

And there she was. The freaking mirage in his head, haunting his every thought. Breaking his concentration with distressing regularity.

He'd buried himself in work. Half a world away, so he didn't have to see Anya's dry-eyed broken face.

He'd succeeded in winning half the battle.

The work was fulfilling, giving him a newfound purpose and challenge he'd not felt for the last two years.

But he couldn't get rid of the image of Anya. The last look he'd had of the woman he'd married in such unholy haste it appalled him now.

She'd not cried. She'd not made a fuss when she'd come to know of Aster's devilish machinations.

No, she'd just left him. Right in the office where he'd been driven to heaven inside her.

When his head was disordered chaos so he'd not been able to form a single coherent thought. And fucking Aster had shown up and *ruined* everything.

Worse, a million times more worse, was the idea that Aster hadn't ruined everything.

He had.

When he'd set this whole game into motion, just to get his hands on Chan Holdings, a crucial part of The Verdant Fund project.

But this wasn't what haunted him. The idea that that he'd used Anya, exploited her situation to his own selfish gains although that was just one of the many perfidies he'd committed when it came to Anya Mallya-Bhatt.

He'd touched her. He'd *consumed* her with no finesse whatsoever because he'd been too far gone when he'd seen her in his workspace.

He'd taken her innocence on his fucking office chair.

He'd not noticed the stain of blood on him, in the aftermath of Aster dropping that damned check off and Anya running away from him like she'd discovered he was a serial killer.

But when he'd taken a brisk shower in the bathroom she'd vacated mere minutes ago, he'd discovered a small red trail on himself.

And he'd howled like a fucking animal, the sound reverberating in the confines of the bathroom.

Exactly, what he was.

He decided he'd stay the hell away from her for the duration of their arrangement. All three months of it. It was the only thing he could do for her.

The only thing she'd asked of him.

He'd succeeded for exactly ten days. Each of which he'd spent working himself into exhaustion, but unable to rid himself of the magnitude of his own guilt.

Each day he worked out deals, placed more pieces of the excellent presentation Mili kept sending him. And convinced more people to come onboard The Verdant Fund. It was some of her best work.

And each night, he watched the seconds tick by on his phone.

His thumb hovering on Anya's number. But he never pressed call on it. He never could.

So what if he couldn't control his own brain from conjuring hot and febrile images of Anya on his desk, in his bed, warm, willing, and *his*…any more than he could short the NASDAQ 500 ticker on a bad tip.

So what if Aster Chan's cursed prophecy had come true and he bitterly regretted tangling with her and his new bride…

She hated him. He deserved it. The least he could do was give her the space so she could hate him in peace. And, when it was all over, she'd be a wealthy woman in her own right and he'd consider it his penance.

Except, Dev had given him the opening he needed. The one he so desperately needed he'd snatched at it without thinking, his brain already making the connection to the end result without him being aware of it.

An excuse to see Anya. Talk to Anya.

To touch her and assure himself she was real.

Mili sent him a thumbs up emoji for the Anya message and he was half-convinced she wouldn't come. Just to spite him.

~ ~ ~ ~ ~ ~

But, here she was. Alighting from the jet in a private airfield off O'Hare Airport. In a severe cut, tight-fitting plum-colored skirt that brushed past her knees. She wore a pistachio silk shell that left her arms bare and a large hat, of all things, her crazy, unruly hair tucked into it.

Drake didn't know what to name the feelings running riot inside him. All he knew was that the sky was bluer, the air lighter, he could *breathe* better with every step she took down the flight stairs.

"Close your mouth, Mr. Fallahil," the man hired to be his guard murmured. "You're drooling."

Drake whipped on his glasses and gave the man a droll look. "I'm not paying you to be cheeky with me, McRae."

Shane McRae, a bright star with Sagitta Consulting - a security outfit bar none - and a former Marine sniper to boot, whipped his own glasses on and assumed the standard bodyguard's pose. Hands laced in front, back at the ready for any threat.

With his dark looks, he looked like a big, tough motherfucker in a fancy suit.

"Sorry, sir," Shane murmured. "I'll think twice before employing cheek with you again."

A muscle twitched in Drake's cheek because he heard an undercurrent of amusement in his bodyguard's tone.

But before he could retort something cutting or *fire* the man, Anya stood in front of him.

One of the flight staff rolled by with one of those gold-plated hotel luggage trollies, piled high with monogrammed luggage from the world's most expensive brand. There were at least seven bags in there.

For a two-day trip.

It seemed a little excessive, but what did he know of women's fashion.

Drake opened his mouth to say something, anything. Instead, he removed his glasses so he could devour every remembered inch of her.

Damnably, her wide-brimmed hat covered her face and tickled his nose.

But, her smell was the same. Warm, enticing woman.

His fingers itched, *hurt* to touch her.

Anya leaned up and kissed his stubbled cheek. "Hello, darling husband. Did you miss me?"

THREE

Anya dropped back to her feet, on shoes that pinched her toes and cramped them into tiny pained bits.

She kept her composure with effort, because being this close to Drake was unnerving, to say the least. And damaging to her psyche if she chose to acknowledge it.

Drake snaked one arm to her elbow and touched her. "Would you believe it, if I said, yes, dear wife?"

Anya felt the touch lick fire up and down her hand. And she believed, sincerely, it was rage fueling the fire.

She'd somehow convinced herself he wasn't as impactful in the two weeks since she'd last seen him. Because she only remembered his face with that flicker of true anguish before it had become a ruthless mask, so it was easy to think that.

Reality, though, was something else.

Drake was overwhelming. His jaw was squarer than it had ever been, the hair waving gently as if celestial air was allowing it to do so. His shoulders were larger than they'd ever been in the olive green shirt, which he wore simply. No jacket, in deference to the balmy Chicago morning.

He'd chosen grey flat-front pants to go with the shirt and the slim belt on his waist was…

Anya looked down. She did not want to remember what it felt like to have that belt hissing through belt loops when she discarded it.

"You're right." She chuckled. "I don't believe you."

His hand gripped her elbow for a fraction of a second before he let go entirely.

She was masochistic because she felt deprived of his touch for a moment. Then, sanity kicked in and she focused her attention on discomfiting him.

Anya deliberately brushed her power-backed shoulders against his. "And who is the brooding handsome?" She winked at the man who wore a full suit in the baking summer heat. He was handsome in that smooth way she did not find attractive, although he was as tall as Drake, inch for inch. "And can I have him?"

Drake gave her a tight smile, which stretched the lines of his eyes all over his face. "That's Shane McRae. He's providing security for us when we are here. In America."

"Oh my gosh." Anya clucked, placing one elegantly manicured hand over her chest so her boobs jutted out in prominence. "Is he our bodyguard?"

FUCK. She sounded like a clueless moron.

Drake nodded. "Yeah. He is. His job is to protect you. Keep you safe."

"Oh yeah?" Anya licked her plum-colored lips, felt the texture of the lip color on her tongue. "He can keep me anytime he wants."

Shane McRae's generous lips tightened and he whipped off his shades to reveal eyes that were, if possible, even grimmer than Drake's. His were a hellacious black and with just as much fire in them.

"It would be my duty, ma'am," he drawled.

Anya immediately tossed all ideas of messing with the bodyguard to further her cause and focused on the object of her detestation.

~ ~ ~ ~ ~ ~

"So, Caleb. Are we going to bake on this tarmac forever?" She pointed at the trolley which contained all sixteen of her outfit changes for this wedding weekend. Complete with shoes, accessories, even underwear and Spanx. "If so, I'd love to change into my Standing on Tarmac outfit. This hat is a little too much for this one, no?"

She cocked her head and regarded Drake.

"I'm not Caleb," Drake said shortly.

"But you are," she protested innocently. "It says so in the marriage certificate. Caleb Drake Fallahil wedded to Anya Mallya-Bhatt."

Drake's jaw hardened.

She noticed the way the corners of his cheekbones clenched. It filled her with vicious pleasure.

"Caleb's my father's name." He spoke in a lethally soft tone. "Not mine. I'm Drake. Okay?"

"Ouch. Touchy, aren't we?" Anya took her life in her hands and poked at his rigid bicep with one fake nail. The muscle there did not give.

She felt a low trembling in the pit of her stomach. Attributed it to adrenalin from sparring with him. And winning.

"The car, Shane?" Drake bit off in the bodyguard's direction.

Shane nodded. "This way, ma'am, sir."

He took them through a tiny hangar that would not house the wingspan of the enormous Gulfstream she'd ridden in, on a solo Transatlantic flight. One, under normal circumstances, she'd have enjoyed the hell out of. But she'd spent the hours on this particular flight, alternatively seething and snoozing. Or working on the last leg of the Verdant Fund proposal.

Shane loped toward a parked unmarked electric SUV and opened the passenger door. He even held out a hand for her to get into the car.

Anya had to hitch the stupid skirt higher so she could climb the high step on the car. She gave him a grateful smile, adjusting the angle of her hat so it did not bump into the roof and almost collapsed on the backseat.

Drake, of course, got in with an economy of movement. It shouldn't have been hot but when that many muscles on a corded thigh moved, she had to look.

"It's unfair, you know," she commented lightly. "What the world makes women go through to call them beautiful. High heels. Bras. Super tight skirts that make our knees itch."

She touched a hand to her super-flat belly, fully aware that both men were staring at her. "Spanx." She gave them a wide-toothed smile. "So worth it, isn't it?"

Shane inclined his head, but not before she caught the glimpse of a smile on his lips. He shut the door on both their faces.

Finally, it was just her and Drake. Alone. In the confines of a moving vehicle. And she could smell him, that woodsy aftershave she'd smelled on herself for days afterward. Just as she'd found his marks on her thighs, her hips, her breasts.

And despised herself for tracing them on her skin as if she could *ever* like it that he'd touched her.

"Seven bags?" He asked her finally.

"Hmmm?" She was so lost in thought she didn't hear his question.

"Did you buy out Changi's duty-free before boarding the flight? What exactly do you have seven bags for?"

Anya removed her hat, allowed her hair to settle around her shoulders.

Drake looked determinedly out the tinted glass windows. But she knew, oh she knew, he could see her reflection on the glass. So she shook her shoulders once.

"Well, since all your assistant told me about this wedding was that it was mandatory, without giving any more clues as to what outfits I'd need to wear, I came prepared as such."

"I see."

"I suppose you do."

Drake whipped off his glasses then and she wanted to shrink into the seat to get away from the force of his glare. It was nuclear, incendiary, like a spotlight lit his eyes, burning away all feeling from it. Leaving only quiet ruthless in it.

This man was not civil. No matter how he pretend to be.

And she *hated* that about him.

"I admire your commitment to the role of blushing bride but we're alone now, Anya. You can be yourself now."

Anya's hands clenched. His eyes dropped to her knees and she crossed her legs, drawing his line of sight to the length of her thighs, instead of her shaking hands.

"Oh, but I am, Mr. Fallahil," she said sweetly. "I'm wearing Prada couture, and Jimmy Choo accessories. The finest your special Amex could buy in all of Orchard Street. Your bride I may be, appearing on command as specified by the terms of our contract, but blushing I'm not."

"Anya, I'm sor--"

She made a slashing motion with her hand. "I don't care for your apology."

Drake swallowed, his Adam's apple moving slow with the motion.

Anya had a sudden vision of reaching over and kissing his throat. Right on the Adam's apple. And then moving down to that intriguing patch of skin she was obsessed with.

If he'd been halfway decent, halfway human, she would have. Relationships, even transactional ones, were built on less than sex.

"Will you give me one second to explain?" He sounded so tired. As if he *really* wanted to explain what had happened on a night that should have been unforgettable for her.

It was, but for vastly different reasons.

She gave him the coolest glance she could muster. "What's there to explain, sir? You used me to win ten million dollars from some chick obsessed with you. Correct me if I'm wrong?"

Drake stared at her, while the car moved at a steady clip.

Her heart thudded so evenly, she could almost believe she wasn't affected by him. He was just another man. He was no one to her. She could hurt him, make him pay, and move on.

Then he shook his head, a lightning fast emotion changing his eyes, dimming them before leaving his face mercurially blank. "Don't call me sir. I'm not your boss."

She felt the reaction like a punch to her gut. "No," she agreed. "I'm your unpaid intern. You're not even the boss of me."

"Anya, please," he tried again.

"No," she cut in. "I am here," she continued with quiet venom. "As ordered by you. Via *text*. To your assistant. I am going to do my duty and be your bride while your sister-in-law gets married."

"Sister's sister-in-law," he corrected.

"Right. Whatever." She waved a hand. "Whoever. I'm going to do what you've asked. To the letter. And no more. You can try to make me do more."

The smile she gave him was as vicious as any he'd ever given her. Full of unnamed power and triumph. "I really hope you do."

He put on his glasses then in a slow, precise movement.

"Thank you," he said formally. His voice rusty with some emotion she couldn't name, his expression hidden from her. "For showing up anyway. I'm in your debt for it. But I was curious about one thing."

"What?" She couldn't believe the ache in her throat.

"If I had called you, messaged you…asked you to come here with me in person, would you have?"

Now, it was Anya's turn to jam the hat over her head so her face was hidden from him. She turned her head to the window for good measure as disappointment ached like a living thing in her heart. "But you didn't. So you'll never know, will you?"

FOUR

"What are you doing, Anya?" Drake knocked on the door of Anya's suite, the next morning. He'd known she'd not stay with him and, truth be told, he wasn't sure he could share a room or bed with her either.

It hadn't been easy the few days they had been together because she was so…unobtrusive. And freakishly neat about picking up after herself.

Now, that he knew what it was to have her, to slide into her slick warmth, it was next to impossible.

Although the knowledge that she was right there, next door to him, in the same freaking continent as him had made him drink copious amounts of Mescal and hammer the last details of The Verdant Fund in place. He just needed government approval from seventeen countries and he could set the whole plan in motion.

"What are you doing?" He knocked again. "We need to leave in five minutes." He spoke the rest of his thought in an undertone. "And then I can send you back and suffer in peace."

His phone buzzed. Drake frowned. He'd instructed Mili to intercede comms on his behalf so who would be calling him.

It was Shane McRae's boss, Rowan. The owner of the security agency he used when he was traveling. The man had sent a single text.

Attached is the file on Anya Mallya-Bhatt. And all known associates. Check out the section on the Runwals, should be of particular interest to you. – Rowan.

He'd retained Sagitta to do a deep background on his wife, for business, he'd told himself. But the truth was, he was intrigued by her, far more than he was comfortable admitting.

Drake replied with a simple thanks, man. And was about to swipe the file open when the door to the suite opened with a swish.

Out stepped a woman who'd put Morticia Adams to shame.

~ ~ ~ ~ ~

She was all in black. Her figure-hugging dress was a severe crow's color sucking the light out of the room. Her eyes were lined a pitch black with hectic gold on her rounded cheeks. She wore some sort of black stone on her ears, dangling down like a witch's crucible.

Today, she'd opted to leave her curls open so they swirled around her shoulders. The ends highlighted a ludicrous purple.

And her lips, Jesus Christ, was that *black* lipstick on her sexy fuckable lips?

Those lips curved, slightly, ironically when she took in his appearance. It was a friend's wedding so he'd cleaned up and wore an Armani tux in midnight black, an exact compliment to her outfit. Now that he thought about it.

"Don't you wear the fuck out of that suit, Mr. Fallahil?"

Drake took a step back as he gazed at his new wife in her funereal outfit.

Anya struck a pose, hand on her waist, hip cocked out, laying the other on the doorjamb. Something sparkled on her slender hand, almost weighing it down.

"I've upgraded my jewelry. You like?" She waggled her fingers at him.

And he stared, mesmerized at the way her lips moved under the heavy black lipstick.

She blew him a kiss through pursed lips, picked up a vintage Judith Lieber clutch done in black cabochon diamonds, and slinked away. Her wrap was a black sable blend she draped around her arms, as if she was cold in perfect summer weather.

Anya turned and winked at him, the purple highlights glinting in the hotel lobby. "Are you coming? We don't want to be late, right?"

Drake could only watch as her pert ass swayed in a strut over devil-red heels designed for only one purpose. To make a man salivate and go down on his knees.

He wondered what she'd do if he ripped the damn dress off, slammed her against the door of this elegantly-appointed hotel corridor and fucked her with those shoes on.

Drake shook his head, allowing the red haze of inconvenient desire and acute anger at her provocation to recede from his usually cool head. It wasn't easy but he managed it. Barely.

When he caught up with her, she'd already joined Shane at the elevator.

He gave the impassive bodyguard a single speaking glance. "Take the stairs, Shane."

Anya cocked her head, quizzically. "Why would he do that? Isn't he supposed to guard my body in case something happened to me in this elevator?"

Drake pursed his lips. "I'll guard your body in this elevator. Shane, stairs. Please."

Shane nodded, gave Anya a small smile and vacated the elevator.

Anya stood to one side of the elevator when Drake stepped in, rejection telegraphed clear by the rigid lines of her body.

"I'm not even going to pretend to understand why you're dressed like you're going to a funeral," Drake began ruminatively.

"Can't you?" She gave him a disbelieving look. "How do I not know your sister's sister-in-law is not a Satanist who enjoys a little Criss Angel? It's not like you deigned to share any details with me."

"You could have asked," he snapped back.

"I could have…" Her voice shook, her eyes flashed as if lit by an internal fire.

He felt a corresponding heat in his own body. Right where his cock started stirring to stubborn, inconvenient life.

"You're lucky I haven't set fire to your fucking penthouse, Mr. Fallahil," she whispered furiously. "All I did was throw your money on clothes that could only have been designed by a man because they are absolute torture to wear."

She stood on one leg, extracted the devil-red shoe which had a horn-like twist to the toe. She held it like it was a weapon. And it was - the thing was pointed on both ends.

Drake took a wary step back. Who knew if she really did have it in her to wield the damn thing?

"This cost you twenty thousand Singapore dollars. I hope you hate me for it. And I hope you're bloody satisfied. "

"I don't hate you," Drake muttered. "And as for being satisfied…Not even close, woman."

He wanted to touch her. Hold her. Do *something* with all that was pinging inside of him, like little bolts of electric current stimulating his blood until all he could do was…

Drake jerked her close. Wary of the murder weapon shoe, but uncaring too.

Anya pressed the sharp heel against his chest, where the damn tuxedo jacket had come open. It ground against his skin, pricking through the pristine white shirt he wore underneath with, dammit, black cabochon diamonds.

Anya looked possessed, as she pressed the heel in deeper into him.

Her eyes focused on the patch of skin she was hurting.

~ ~ ~ ~ ~

His own were focused on her intent expression, visible even through the concrete layer of makeup she wore. He caressed her elbows, the heat and warmth of her warming his palms. Tingling them into life.

"Anya," he whispered.

"Don't say my name," she shot back. The heel was almost digging into his skin. "You have no right to say it."

"I know," he said in a low voice. "I know I have no right to anything. But I'm begging you, Anya. Please, let me apologize and explain what happened the other night."

"I won't believe you," she hurled back.

"Is this what you want then?" He trapped the shoe against his chest, allowed it to sink in enough to penetrate his skin. "I always tell the truth, but you want to see me bleed?"

Her lips gasped open in shock. She violently shook off his hold and stepped back, careening to the other end of the elevator.

"I don't want to see you bleed. Holding that kind of grudge is a Fallahil specialty, isn't it?" She tossed the bitter, acrimonious words out as she struggled into her shoe.

"Please," he said, a third time. "Will you listen to me?"

Anya gave him a scornful look. "I'm stuck in this goddamn elevator with you. For the next three months. What choice do I have?"

Drake took a deep breath and felt his chest rattle from the force of it. He expelled it, trying to bring his chaotic thoughts under some kind of control. The control he was famed for globally.

It wasn't easy when he saw her, his young wife, looking like death warmed over on a bad day. And knowing he'd done this to her. He knew then what he had to do.

He had to tell her the ugly truth.

"Aster Chan comes from a long line of business owners who hold valuable connections in the government here and in countries all over Asia."

"So?" She was suspicious.

"So, we were involved for a brief time when I first moved to Singapore."

"You mean she fell in love with you and you dumped her because you're a cowardly bastard?"

Drake prayed for patience. "I ended things when she inconveniently decided to have feelings for me and pressured me into marrying her. I refused her."

"Why?"

"Because I swore to myself a long time ago, I'd never marry anyone."

She looked disbelieving, rightly so. His wife. "So how did you end up breaking your solemn fucking oath?"

He deserved her scorn. "Unfortunately, as a byproduct of those feelings, her father who I need to do business with was…annoyed with his daughter's choice."

"What are you saying? Robert Chan paid you to marry me to take you off the market for his daughter?"

Drake ran a hand over his jaw. It ached as if he'd gone ten rounds with a champ, when all he'd done was tell her the unvarnished truth. "No. No one paid me any money, Anya. Men in my position, men I work with, we don't deal in money. We deal in secrets, favors. We deal in power."

Anya shook her head. "I believe that. You're all-powerful, aren't you?"

It wasn't a compliment and he knew it.

"My point is," he said, as patiently as he could. "You were a perfect means to the end Robert and I both wanted. Aster gave me three weeks to find a wife, Robert wouldn't lose his daughter and I'd keep my pride."

The golden fire in her expression dulled, turned lackluster. Her face was hard, voice husky when she spoke. "And all you had to do was ruin my life to make it happen, right?"

He gave her a tired look. "Did I really ruin your life, An..?" He clamped his mouth shut. Because she'd told him many times not to say her name. And he'd not earned the right to.

"You withheld the truth from me," Anya listed his sins on her left hand, the damned ring throwing off brilliance. "Maneuvered me into an untenable position where I had no choice but to agree to your feudal agreement. You even went so far as to get my mother operated on, so I'd be eternally grateful to you. You pretended to be nice when you're actually a wolf. And then, you made me want…"

Anya stopped talking.

Her throat worked strongly, as she took in a deep, gulping breath. The movement moved her breasts up and down, and he wanted to cup them. Tug the sweetheart neckline of the sexy dress down and take them into his mouth. Finish this argument in the only way that made sense to him anymore.

Naked. Sweaty. Inside her.

But it was prohibited now.

"I'm sorry," he said slowly. "I'm sorry for the many, *many* things I've done to you. And, for the first time in my life, not that you'll believe me, I think the loss outweighed the win on a deal."

Drake buttoned his jacket so the little wound she'd given him was hidden. Only to be felt by him. "And I'm most sorry that I took your choice of your first sexual experience away from you. You don't have to forgive me. I just wanted you to know. That's all."

"I get it," she said, ticking seconds later. "Why you did what you did. I understand. It was business. And business is all that matters."

He shook his head, expelled another heavy breath. "I...thank you."

"But why am I here, then? Why did you go back on our deal?" She demanded restlessly. "Are you trying to strike a deal with the AllMart people or something?"

"Maybe I missed you enough to break my deal with you?" He retorted, his eyes watchful. Quiet.

"And so you summon me?"

She had a point there.

"Look," he said diffidently.

"No," she cut in swiftly. "You look. Honestly, I don't care about this one-upmanship you one-percenters have going on with each other." Her words hurt way worse than the heel had. "It's above my pay grade. But, I don't like it and I'm not going to pretend otherwise."

"That's fair."

"And as for your apology about the other thing… thank you," she finished stiltedly. "I appreciate it."

"You're welcome."

Anya stabbed the L button for the lobby. "Now can we get this farce over with ASAP? I need to breathe the Spanx out of my body."

He knew he shouldn't grin, so he nodded solemnly. But, in the place where his heart beat, there was a lightness he'd never experienced before. He was unsure what to name it.

He wanted to call it hope.

FIVE

A few hours later, Anya realized there wasn't much difference between the rich getting married versus ordinary middle-class folks.

Sure, the cutlery used at the buffet tables was probably twenty-two carat gold, and the champagne was four-thousand-dollar vintage but…at the heart of it, it was love that drove the ceremony.

And what a beautiful ceremony it was.

The un-Satan-like, totally modern, Hindu wedding of Zara Subramanian and Dev Banerjee was the stuff of romantic fairytales. The white Big Top – called a *shamiana* - tent they'd gathered under, billowed in a gentle summer breeze. The staff was liveried to resemble royal staff and the food…oh, the food was sublime.

Anya'd even interacted with a lovely, heavily pregnant woman named Sophia Kulashreshtha right before the wedding. She was still raw from her last encounter with Drake who'd turned her into a mini monster, and she'd taken it out on the woman kind enough to strike a conversation with her.

It became worse when she discovered who Sophia's husband was. Bharat Shrinivasan had actually been the subject of Anya's graduating thesis, titled – The Fall and Fall of India's Bad Boy of Tech. Although the big, gruff, dark-haired man Sophia kept smiling looked nothing like a bad boy businessman.

No, he looked besotted with his wife and the mother of his child.

As did the stupidly handsome groom, Dev.

When he'd danced Zara out of the *mandap*, the traditional altar, and she'd playfully stepped on his toes, he'd whirled her into his arms. Grinning at her as if she was everything. It was hard to believe he was the Chief Operating Officer of a Fortune 500 corporation!

Anya felt struck by the most unexpected and sincere kind of envy. Not for the wedding ceremony itself, or the exquisite arrangements, but the look in the man's eyes. In Bharat's, in Dev's. These powerful, important men had unbent enough to let a woman into their lives, their hearts.

They'd claimed them in holy matrimony because they cared for each other.

There was no manipulation here. No secrets. No desperate agreements with the very devil.

In short, all of these relationships had ended in a beautiful, affirming ceremony.

Her…*thing,* for surely, it was just a thing, with the most enigmatic and confusing man she'd ever met, had begun with a wedding. A lie. And the train wreck had continued ever since.

Maybe I missed you enough to break my deal with you.

He'd said those words so casually. As if he expected her to believe them.

As if she could believe *anything* he ever said, ever again after the things he'd just told her. Using people as casually as if they were pieces on a chess board. No conscience, no compunction, just zeroes on the bottom-line.

But he never lied, the logical side of her brain challenged her.

Drake was many things, none of them good, some of them downright heinous, but he was not a liar. He had no need to.

Then, what could his statement mean?

That he actually missed her? That he cared about *her?* A student nobody from the seedier section of Little India when he lived on the tallest building in all of Singapore?

Anya mentally snorted.

Right. If he cared about her so much why would he have not shared the tiny fact that he had a sister and a nephew whom he loved *very much* with her? One he was no doubt talking to right this minute, having left her alone for the whole damn event!

No. She was just a convenient body for him, a fuckable means to a profitable end.

He'd made his desire of her abundantly clear from minute one. While it was flattering, and made her feel like she had some kind of power over him, she was going to not indulge that particular sin with him.

She'd been the one to pay for it.

~ ~ ~ ~ ~ ~

"Hold that pose," a young woman, maybe her age, in khakhi shorts and an oversize tee instructed her. She held a Leica DSLR in her small hands, with a protruding lens.

She framed it from a distance of three feet, taking Anya's seated position. "Damn. You look powerful." She shot off a quick burst of pictures.

Anya gave her a pleased smile. "Really? I was going for a sort of Victoria Bechkam at Ascot style."

The wedding photographer continued circling her and clicking more pictures. "Nailed it. I fucking love your shoes."

"They're perfect. Aren't they? I had Christian Loubotin's atelier whip it up for me. As a special favor." Anya extended her leg in the torture instruments. The heel of one shoe dangled off her freshly pedicured feet so the skin gleamed.

Only she knew how much she'd winced when the aesthetician at Lux, the premier salon and wellness center in the city, had pumiced her hammer toe the night before she'd boarded the plane. It was just one of the many, many treatments she'd endured so she could look and feel her absolute, empowered best for this event.

"Far out," the photographer commented. She took a picture of Anya's legs in the extended pose. "You're living the dream life, ma'am."

The photographer left with that sincere compliment and a tiny smile on her gamine face. She looked hardly older than Anya, although Anya felt like she'd aged decades in just a few short weeks.

Marriage, she thought philosophically, definitely changed a person.

It had changed Drake too. If the look on his face was any indication when he'd seen her in her wedding finery, he'd shown remarkable constraint limiting himself to just a single scathing comment.

But that look had been priceless.

And he looked so breathtakingly handsome in his own suit with the stupid bowtie and a pocket square that matched the color of her stupid shoes. All Mili's doing, no doubt.

She couldn't fathom, not really, how no woman had ever gotten this man to the altar before her. She could believe, readily, that many might have wanted it, the statucsque Aster Chan included.

To think, she was here with his cumbersome ring on her finger and her head ached. Trying to make sense of it all.

She'd not lied when she said he wore the fuck out of that suit. And, if they had been anything but what they were – enemies bound by a marriage vow – she'd have happily assisted in discarding his suit and enjoyed what she'd been too blinded to, last time.

As it was, he felt *bad* about the only good thing in this arrangement.

It was enough to drive a woman to drink.

So she waved one of the impeccably-dressed staff over. They carried a bucket of champagne. "Yes, ma'am? How can I help you?"

"Can I take the whole bottle?"

The staff nodded, cautiously. "Sure."

Anya stood up, discarding her shoes where she'd sat for the last three hours. Tucked the bottle under her arm and wandered off in the direction of no people, milling about the perfectly manicured lawns of the wedding venue. Into a mansion called Sycamore Drive.

~ ~ ~ ~ ~ ~

Sycamore Drive, Anya surmised, got its name naturally.

The half-mile graveled driveway was flanked with sycamores on either side, which would bloom in just a few days. It was a gorgeous estate in an established part of Chicago, Riverside Heights, a city she'd only seen in movies and TV shows.

But the house she was shamelessly snooping around while swilling expensive Krug, was a home. Well-lived, adored. The well-appointed rooms flowed into one another, the marble Palladian staircase was the right amount of regal.

Even the antique showpieces on the mantelpiece were worn with care.

And the family portrait gracing the wall above the standalone fireplace was *love.*

It showed an old man in a wheelchair, flanked by Dev and Zara in matching green sweaters and Santa hats. On Zara's right was an elegant matriarch in a red sari and a beaming smile on an unlined face. Dev had one arm around a buxom older woman in a curled hairdo, while she gave him a look of utter adoration.

It was the last woman in the portrait who held Anya's attention. She was not as tall as Zara, who looked very queenly with her poker-straight hair and doe-shaped eyes.

But her shoulders were pin-straight and the angle of her jaw, determined and rebellious, reminded Anya of her husband.

She had on a pretty fifties style-dress with Loubotins on her slim feet. She held a tuxedoed boy, with a gap-toothed smile in front of her. She had cornflower blue eyes and sunshine yellow hair hidden under a Santa hat, but her smile was the same as the boy – they were mother and son.

Lily and Bret Fallahil, Anya deduced.

Drake's sister and nephew.

Mili too had never mentioned their existence to Anya and there was no media mention of the two anywhere. Ordinarily, Anya would have concluded this meant Drake did not care about these people, they meant nothing to him.

But she was beginning to think the opposite was true.

That they were the most important people to Drake. Because he'd gone to great lengths to protect their identities.

Unlike her, her logical brain reminded her. He'd never protected her from anything. So she would do well to not take his words seriously.

The thought depressed her. She took another swig from the bottle. It was chilly and tart on her tongue.

~ ~ ~ ~ ~

"So, you're my new aunt." A boyish voice pronounced gravely.

Anya nearly spewed the wine on her Marchessa couture, swallowing it at the last minute. She turned around and saw the grinning boy from the portrait staring guilelessly at her.

He wore a jacket in turquoise blue, his hair was neatly brushed back and he was a foot taller than he'd been at the portrait. He almost came up to her head, especially without the benefit of the heels.

"Are you Bret Fallahil?"

"Soon to be Barranos," he confirmed. Holding his hand out formally.

Anya extended hers. "Well, Bret Fallahil soon to be Barranos. I'm indeed your new aunt." She smiled. "Anya."

"Aunty Anya?"

Anya nodded. "Yeah. I suppose I am. It's very nice to meet you."

"Same." Bret pumped her hand enthusiastically. "My mom says your lipstick is too dark and depressing."

Her lips twitched at Bret's very adult tone. "Your mom's not wrong. It is too dark and depressing. I wanted it to be."

"Why?" Bret was quizzical. "It's Aunty Zara and Uncle Dev's wedding. It's a happy day."

"Yeah." Her smile faded as she realized how childish her actions were that a young man could point out the holes in her logic. "Yes, it is. I should have worn something a bit more cheerful, right?"

"Nah. I like it." Bret shook his head. "My favorite color's black too." He gave her a sharp, sweet grin.

Anya sucked in a stunned breath because she'd seen that precise grin on Drake's face. Exactly once. When he'd bribed the security guards at the Runwals'. A toothy, devilish smile which touched his eyes.

"You, sir, have excellent taste." Anya toasted him with her champagne bottle before guzzling some of it down.

"Mom says you shouldn't drink straight from the bottle." Bret fiddled with the collar of his jacket. "It's bad manners."

His mom sounded like the etiquette police. Anya kept the thought to herself and lowered the bottle. She also kept the question she really wanted to herself.

Did your mom send you here to spy on me?

But before she could say anything else, Bret spied someone else over her shoulder. His eyes widened comically wide, "Uh-oh. My dad's spotted me. I have to go. I wasn't supposed to come check you out."

Then he dashed off giving her a quick sideways hug she was too surprised to return.

Anya almost turned around to see who his dad, this Barranos person was, but someone tapped her on her shoulder.

"Yes?" She said, sticking a polite smile on her face.

Her eyes widened because she stared at an old wizened face. With fading golden hair and piercing blue eyes. They could be a mirror image of Drake's, if they weren't so bloodshot and yellowed at the whites.

"Hello, my dear. You must be my Drake's wife." The old man smiled, exposing yellowing teeth.

His skin was wrinkled and his jaw wasn't as strong or broad as Drake's was, even under the beard. And age or time had shrunk this man's massive presence.

"I must be," Anya murmured, still trying to understand who this man was. Possibilities whirled in her slightly tipsy head.

Surely, he couldn't be –

"My name's Caleb," the old man supplied. "And you were just talking to my grandson, Bret. How he's grown in the last year."

Anya reeled from the revelation. "I…thank you," she said faintly.

"Your beautiful, my dear," her father-in-law complimented her.

Anya could say nothing. She was still trying to process meeting two members of Drake's family in the space of five minutes.

"My son's an idiot for leaving you alone." Caleb's watery eyes drifted down to the bottle in her hand. "To drink."

"He's busy with wedding stuff," Anya said swiftly. Unable to believe she was defending the man she'd vowed to take down.

"That's good for me. Because I need you to do something for me."

She was even more stunned when the man extended a note to her.

"I'd like it very much if you'd pass this note along to Drake. No need to tell him how you got it, if you wouldn't mind." The man gave her a slow, harmless smile. "After all, what's a white lie between family, am I right?"

"I..." Anya accepted the note on reflex.

He gave her a short sharp nod and loped away before she could process what just happened.

She was still staring at the darkness that swallowed Caleb Fallahil, one hand holding the note, the other the champagne bottle when someone else tapped on her shoulder.

"Who's it now?" Anya whirled with an angry mutter.

She paled when she saw who it was.

~~~~~

"Hello, Anya. You left these unattended." A lovely blond woman with quiet blue eyes in a green sari with a golden *zari* border handed her those cursed shoes. She gave a small smile that did not touch her eyes. "They're far too valuable, aren't they?"

"Yes," Anya said thickly. She felt a mixture of acute shame and embarrassment. In her quest to bring Drake down she'd been quite an obnoxious guest here in this woman's home. "I'm sorr--"
~~~~~

"I'm Lily Fallahil," the woman said quickly. "And I'd love to have you over for dinner tonight with…" Drake's sister swallowed, shadows in eyes so unlike her father's and exactly like her brother's.

"Your husband. My brother."

SIX

"Your bride is very…vivacious," Lily observed a few hours later, as she tossed salad greens in a light vinaigrette with the paprika Drake and Kit both loved. She was in the kitchen in Lily's Cottage, where the delicious aromas of yeasty pizza and bubbling cheese filled the air.

Her brother paused in the act of uncorking the wine he'd brought for the occasion. He gave her a chagrined look, looking as unlike himself as Kit had told her he was, after chatting him up before the wedding.

For one, he was dressed down in a simple jacket and trousers with an *unironed* shirt. And he'd run his hand through his beautiful, shades-better-than-her-own-blond hair so it fell in careless waves around his jaw.

"Lily."

"Do you remember how you threatened to beat Kit up when you came to know I wanted him?" she continued stridently. "Unlike you, I'm going to be the bigger person here and not tear you a new one for keeping this from me." She pointed at her chest. "Not this evolved chick."

Whoops could be heard from the living room where Kit, Bret, and the bride were all immersed in an unreleased version of whatever RPG Bret was into that Drake had procured him.

"I'm sorry, Lily." Drake spoke in a rusty voice. Most unlike himself. "For not telling you."

"Is it because it's not real?" Lily asked idly.

She continued mixing the lettuce with the farm-grown cherry tomatoes Kit and Bret had bought in their grocery run while she'd spruced the house up for his brother's wife. No way was she going to allow dust bunnies to spoil Anya's first impression of Lily's Cottage. Or its owner.

Drake gave her a startled look. He finished uncorking the wine and then took a healthy gulp from the bottle.

Lily kept her chuckle to herself. She knew her brother was suffering and it was fun to prolong it. Mostly, because she'd sometimes despaired of Drake ever allowing himself to feel enough *to* suffer. But also, it was fun watching her big brother go to pieces over a woman.

Miracles could happen!

"It's not *not* real," Drake muttered.

Lily was tempted to roll her eyes. But she settled for snatching the wine from him and pouring it into a glass. Like they were civilized people. "Of course, I know that. I'm just teasing you, Drake."

She bumped shoulders with him. Feeling the familiar warmth of family, of self, with him. No matter what happened, what life had become, Drake was her rock. The first father her son had had, and an excellent one at that.

"Can't you take a joke anymore, Mr. One-Percenter?" she teased him gently.

"Don't call me that." Drake flinched. Finished the drink she'd poured him in one gulp. "I need something stronger," he muttered.

He hunted in the cabinets, a big animal in a little room. Gave her a misery-filled look. "Where does Kit keep the good scotch?"

"Not in the kitchen where a curious twelve-year-old can find them, Drake," Lily said gently. "Are you okay? You look…" Undone. *Crazy.*

Drake's face hardened, turned into the cool mask she hated. The one he wore when he was in the middle of a conference or meeting with business associates. The one he'd never had cause to use around her.

"How do I look, dearest Lils?" He gave her a smile which turned his lines into deep brackets around his eyes. And made mock of her question for daring to ask him.

"Never mind. Let's just eat, shall we?" Lily made to lift the salad bowl when Drake pushed it down.

"Can you sit down for a second? I need to talk to you."

She'd have teased him a lot longer, but he sounded so…defenseless. Vulnerable even. She knew Drake. It was the last thing he'd ever choose to be. So whatever this was, it was important.

Lily drew Drake to the breakfast nook and pushed him into a seat. Then she perched on a stool next to him, bringing the wine with her.

"Talk," she ordered.

"Where do I start?" He was adorably perplexed.

"From the beginning?" Lily suggested.

Drake stared unseeingly at the bottle she held. And then said the most unexpected thing ever. "Then, I guess I have to tell you that Caleb…my dad's back."

The bottle almost slipped out of Lily's nerveless fingers but Drake caught it. He gave her a wan smile that did nothing to dispel the shock of his statement.

"You can't be serious."

"As the Nasdaq Top 50, Lils. He found me after I shifted to Singapore. This nightmare gossip blogger, whom I can't find, leaked the fact that I'd moved there. That's how he contacted me."

Lily's breath gasped out of her chest. "Why did you fire your PR people again?"

"I didn't fire them," Drake protested. "I just didn't think I needed them anymore."

"Clearly, brother. You were wrong. And now your *dad* is back in our lives."

"He's not back in our lives." He squeezed her hand. "I'm keeping him away from us. From you. From Bret. I swear to you, Lils. The man's not coming anywhere near my kid."

The weak and childish part of her mind, where only instinct and memory lived, flashed back to a time when the days were dark and a man with a booming voice and whiskey-laden scent scared her into nightmares every night. And every night, every night, without fail Drake had shushed her into better dreams. Holding her till the nightmares were banished.

Now, she knew how he'd done it. At the cost of himself.

Because adult Lily could recall the slickness on his back and know it was blood.

Her brother was *everything* to her and she'd become everything she was because of him. There weren't enough words in the dictionary to describe how much she loved him.

Her lips trembled. It was all the weakness Lily allowed herself. "I know that. You're Drake. You won't let the monsters hurt us."

Drake nodded, the fires of holy hell burning in his haunted eyes. Eyes so unlike hers and yet were, at the same time. "I'm the biggest baddest monster there is. So you're safe."

And because it was Drake and he never ever lied to her, she believed him. She was safe. Her son, her world was safe. That didn't mean…

~ ~ ~ ~ ~

"But are you?" Lily asked softly.

He was about to nod, she knew it. Knew her brother's instinctive response was to control it. To not share his troubles and sorrows with anyone. Drake was the oldest, the most responsible and he'd had to take care of her in their shared miserable childhood.

As an adult, he'd made himself into a stone fortress which let no one in.

"I was…I thought I was. But now I think, I'm thrown, Lily," he admitted rawly. "I've made so many mistakes and missteps that I don't know anymore."

More whoops could be heard from the living room. One of them was a slight female voice, singing some kind of a victory song.

"Is *she* one of those missteps, Drake?" Lily pointed in the direction of the living room. "Was that why she looked so terribly upset today?"

Drake hung his head and, for the first time, since Lily had gained consciousness she saw her brother, her rock, the surest thing in her world hunched into himself. She wondered if even he knew how defenseless he looked.

"I don't know anymore. It was supposed to be a business deal with her. Well, with Aster's dad. But now...I..."

"Wait. What?" Lily interrupted, bemused. "Who's Aster's Dad? How is he involved in your marriage?" Her eyes widened. "Please don't tell me Anya's some human trafficking victim. I can't..."

"What? No!" Drake exploded. "Jesus, Lily. Who do you think I work with?"

Lily sipped at her own wine slowly, feeling it coat her throat with courage and blessed warmth. "Since I started taking an interest in AllMart I'm beginning to better understand how you high net worth individuals actually, you know, keep your net worth so high. You do whatever it takes."

Drake nodded instantly. "I did. I do," he sounded unapologetic. "It's the only way I know to keep...us safe."

She knew he wanted to say myself. But he didn't. Because to admit that would be admitting vulnerability. She let him get away with it.

"But I've looked into AllMart and Kit's Enter the Dragon and their business practices are above reproach, Lils. You can rest your conscience easy with them," he said earnestly.

Of course her brother had her new family investigated and checked out. Right down to their personal credit lines and favorite ice cream flavor. She raised one brow and said, "Can you say the same about your own business practices?"

"I could," Drake argued. "But then…" He trailed off, took a deep breath and unloaded a fantastic tale on Lily.

One where a party was held in an upscale penthouse and an alleged call girl was caught trying to steal valuable information from a competitor. And Drake's ex bet him ten million dollars to find a wife or be run out of town like a cowardly dog. And *her* father offered him an even sweeter deal to marry anyone else other than his daughter.

Lily's eyes rounded and her jaw dropped, almost to the floor by the time Drake finished narrating it all.

"So, let me get this straight," she said faintly. "Anya's actually a brilliant MBA student on scholarship she can't afford to lose, so you should have helped her with her mom's medical issues. Instead, you blackmailed Anya into marrying you to close a billion-dollar deal while also winning ten million from your less-than-stable ex."

"That's it in a nutshell." He looked critically at the almost-finished bottle of Merlot. "We need more wine, don't we?"

"I need a freaking bar to process all this, Drake," Lily declared. She poked him with the sharp edge of her wine glass. "What the fuck were you thinking, playing with people's lives like that?"

"I was trying to save my business. My legacy," Drake protested. "Bret's legacy."

"Oh, don't you dare emotionally blackmail me, Drake. This is about you," Lily whispered furiously. "Your need for control. To outwit the people who tried to manipulate you by winning every single aspect of this wretched game you were playing."

He winced. "Lily."

"And you used that poor, innocent woman to do it all," Lily concluded. "No wonder she is pissed *off*. If I were her I'd make you pay a hundred times for your transgressions."

Drake's lips twitched. "She bought a twenty thousand dollar pair of shoes to spite me. I think she has that covered."

"She's not thinking big enough. I'm going to talk to her and give her some ideas," Lily said, "And you should be ashamed of yourself, Drake. You've always been ruthless but this crosses the line."

He shrugged. "I don't know any other way to be."

~ ~ ~ ~ ~

Kit came in whistling, holding his hands up. He wore his at-home jeans and a blue tee shirt which had officially spent more time in her washer than his. A fact which pleased her ridiculously.

"I've been sent to ask about victuals," Kit said. "The final battle royale's about to commence and the warriors are famished."

At Drake's perplexed look he translated, "Pizza. We need pizza and fries."

"Right. Pizza."

"It's going to be five minutes, honey." Lily leaned up and gave Kit an absent kiss. "Can the troops survive?"

"Sure." He gave her a soft look that never failed to melt her inside out. "You're okay, love?"

She nodded. "I am." And she was. Because she had him and Bret and her pig-headed, utterly stupid brother. "But I need five minutes with Drake. Sibling talk. You get it, don't you?"

Kit gave her shoulder a reassuring squeeze and left the room, nodding at Drake.

"You know he wants to buy you a bigger house. He doesn't fit in here," Drake commented stridently. He gave Kit's massive departing back an appraising glance. "I'm surprised he's put up with using that Japanese schoolgirl toilet in your bedroom for the last year."

"What?" Lily's eyes widened again. "How did you know we've been looking at houses?"

Now it was Drake's turn to chuckle at her expense. "Why do you think I'm here, sis? Kit wants my expert opinion on which property is best suited for your family needs. Since you won't offer, you know." He leaned his back against the wall. "An opinion."

She gave him the finger to wipe the smug smile off his beloved face. "I like where we are. It's home."

"It is," Drake agreed idly. "But your home's… expanded. So changing houses is the expedient course of action, isn't it?"

Lily bit her lip. Considered the faded wallpaper that this supremely confident and seriously wealthy man had helped her hang, seven years ago when she'd first moved to Chicago. Bret had been five and she'd wanted to give him a sense of home, of family…and get away from her overbearing and controlling brother.

It was hard to remember Drake's identity in the real world when she only knew him as her brother.

"It's hard to give up a part of me, Drake," she demurred. "This house turned me into an adult. How can I just leave it and go?"

"So, don't, Lily." Drake looked at the miniscule kitchen where they'd prepared seven Christmas dinners. "I'll keep it safe for you."

"You really would, won't you?" She was moved to tears by the almost casual offer of help he'd just made her. Even though he meant every single word.

Drake gave her a dead earnest look. "I'd do anything for you, Lily. Do you even have to ask?"

Lily swallowed and kissed his hard cheek. "Then find a way to un-Drake this mess you've created. Be less ruthless. Talk to Anya," she suggested quietly. "For better or worse or business, she's your wife. You owe her that much at least."

It surprised her that he did not immediately refute any of her suggestions. And, if the thoughtful, focused look on his masked face was any indication, he was considering them.

That was unexpected, wonderful progress.

Maybe, Lily thought with a sudden spurt of hopeless romanticism, there was more to this arrangement than even Drake realized. She couldn't wait to see it unfold for her brother!

He deserved all the love in the world even though he'd never ask for it.

SEVEN

Dinner at the Fallahil-Barranos household, Anya discovered, was a raucous affair.

Lily's Cottage was a warm lovely slice of domesticity with miniscule rooms that could not possibly contain Kit's bulk. The cottage was as unlike the exclusive Trident Atrium as it was possible for a home to be.

Drake too looked at home here, sprawled full-length beneath the couch, resting against it.

The Barranos boys, for Bret was undoubtedly trying to imitate his tough-looking adoptive dad, were easygoing and friendly for the most part.

Bret talked a lot, giving his favorite and attentive uncle the rundown on all that he'd accomplished in the last week since they'd spoken. He wore basketball shorts and a jersey three sizes too big for him.

Apparently, it was a classic, belonging to Magic Jordan himself. Kit and Drake had gifted it to him together for his birthday.

He'd shared that little fact three times with her already.

Kit was a wonderful father, Anya figured. Although she couldn't understand why the profit-monger would blow thousands of dollars on making a young boy happy.

Kit offered casual pointed remarks designed to needle Drake and tease Bret, but he meant no harm. He was faultlessly nice. Even though he looked every inch the ex-MMA fighter he was. And his odd-colored eyes positively melted every time they landed on his fiancée, Lily.

Lily Fallahil was a gentle ruler of the world she created. What she said, was gospel.

Even, Anya realized with a small pang, for Drake.

For instance, she'd told Drake to have more of the salad and less pizza slices and the man listened.

It was fascinating.

Anya knew Lily was skeptical about her. That she was withholding judgment about Anya herself but her hostess skills were flawless. She made sure Anya's wine glass was filled, gave her the meatier parts of the pizza and specially double tissue-dipped her portion of the fries.

Anya couldn't pinpoint how, but it felt like Lily had unbent towards her in some way. Especially because she'd not been anything more than polite and cordial to her.

~ ~ ~ ~ ~ ~

"Mom, Uncle Drake and I are going to play a quick game of hoops before dessert. We promised each other, didn't we?" Bret gave his mom a heart-melting smile.

"Sure, thing, baby. Kit you're going to join them?" Lily brushed a hand over her son's tousled head. He leaned into her touch for a loving second before moving back to Drake's side.

"I don't think Barranos has it in him to take on both me and the squirt, does he?" Drake smiled broadly.

"No." Kit burped behind his large hand. Gave her a self-conscious smile. "Excuse me, Anya."

"That's alright, Kit." Anya gave a louder burp from where she was sitting cross-legged on the recliner. "Air must come out or it will find a way to."

Lily chuckled and Bret burst out laughing at her slightly off-color comment. Kit toasted her with his beer bottle while Drake calmly munched on a celery stick. No reaction visible on his ruggedly handsome face.

He'd been strangely quiet for the ride back from Sycamore Drive, through changing outfits and driving here. It was the main reason she'd tucked Caleb's note in her purse and not given it to him yet.

If she didn't know better, she'd think he was actually sad. But she did know better; so she understood he was just being Drake.

He had no further use for her right now so there was no point engaging with her.

She was glad, Anya told herself. She was glad he had nothing more to say to her. For she wouldn't listen to a word he said.

"Then it's settled." Drake stood up in a fluid position, his shirt riding up to reveal a patch of tanned ribbed stomach. Heat curled inside Anya, unwilling and undeniable.

He casually held Bret under one arm, swinging him in the air.

The boy shrieked in delight, even though it was probably unhealthy to do that when he'd just eaten.

"I'm going to drub the kid into oblivion." Drake gave Kit a formal smile. "Kit, you'll referee?"

Lily and Kit had a weird couples-only conversation. All eyes and unreadable facial expressions.

Anya was fascinated by it, as she'd been by everything she'd seen tonight.

Especially Drake.

This was a side of Drake she'd never expected existed, much less see. Watching Drake talk long division and equations with Bret and actually pay attention to him made Anya understand why he'd buy Bret a Magic Johnson jersey. Or buy him an unreleased beta of the latest League of Legends. Or call him every week.

It's because he loved the boy. Sincerely and without reservations.

This was no act. There was no deal.

He was just an uncle playing with his nephew.

It was a blow to her already fragile heart.

Because it meant he *was* different. He was decent. When he chose to be.

~ ~ ~ ~ ~

"I think I'm going to let Lily take point on this one," Kit said slowly, glancing at Anya. Who had a wistful look on her mobile face that she wasn't even unaware of. "Lily you up for it?"

Bret clapped. "Come on, you guys. Time's wasting."

Drake and Bret and Lily departed the living room, leaving Kit and Anya alone. He stretched a bit before picking up the empty pie plates on the low-slung dining table in one hand. "Can I get you anything else, Anya?"

Anya shook her head. She gathered the plates and cups and cutlery they'd used, careful to leave Drake's stuff where it was. "No. I'm stuffed. I'll do the dishes. It will work all this greasy food off."

"My mama would approve of that. Thanks so much, Anya."

Kit preceded her into the tiny kitchen and showed her where everything was.

Pretty soon, she was elbow deep in sudsy warm water, scraping the remains of their meal and cleaning the mess.

He stood at the edge of the counter. A respectful distance away. But the kitchen was such a tiny space and Kit was six-three and more than two hundred pounds easy that his presence was immense. Unmissable.

"So, you're getting your MBA at NUS?" He asked idly.

"Yeah. I am. I'll graduate next spring."

"That's amazing, congratulations."

"Thanks." She gave him a pleased smile. "I've seen some of your live-stream events. You were *hot* in twenty-twelve."

"I'm not hot now?" Kit winked his green eye at her. The brown one twinkled with general contentment.

"I'm reasonably sure you did not put away four slices of homemade deep dish in twenty-twelve." She slid around his clever question. "You had an elite athlete's diet back then, didn't you?"

"I lived for cheat days," he confessed. "I can understand why your husband's impressed with you. You've a remarkable brain."

"My husb…" She cleared her throat because the phrase sent a helpless little thrill rushing through her. "Drake's not impressed with me."

"I've not known that man to do anything without being a hundred percent certain of and impressed by it," Kit confided. "Especially when it comes to his personal life. He married you, Anya. He's impressed with you."

"You know Drake well, don't you?" She murmured.

Kit shook his head. "God, no. Every time he and I come within ten feet of each other, he wants to murder me." He spoke with real feeling.

"Does he?" Her lips twitched. "Why?"

"Because no one is good enough for his baby sister. And I dared to be worthy of her."

"That sounds…nice," she said softly.

"It is," he agreed. "Until all that anger is directed at you and you are at the receiving end of one of his slick ultimatums."

"Tell me about it," Anya said feelingly.

"You know, he tried to threaten me with buying out my business when he first found out about Lily and me?" Kit confided.

"He threatened to shut down the bank where all my savings were deposited if I didn't marry him," Anya shot back.

Kit straightened, startled. He folded his impressive arms, his biceps bulging under the oxford shirt he wore. And there was a distinctly feral look in his changeable eyes. "He did what?"

Anya finished scrubbing the last of the cups and placed it in the dishwasher. "But, I'm beginning to think…he wouldn't have done that to me. To those people at the bank. Not really."

She gave him a look over her shoulder, bent at the waist. "Would he?"

Kit hesitated.

"Anya," he said slowly. "Do you need help? Drake might be filthy rich, but I can protect you from him if need be."

Anya giggled, even though tears flooded her throat at his earnest offer. "You're a hero, aren't you, Kit Barranos? A regular Captain America." She shook her head before he could press his point. "But I don't need protecting from Drake. In fact, if anything, the opposite is true."

She dried her hands on the soft towel hanging on the dishwasher handle. And slid on the bling ring she'd taken off for the chore.

"I plan on making a considerable dent in his portfolio for trying to control me. How's that for payback?" Anya waggled her hand.

Kit whistled, suitably impressed. "You really are smart, you know. You figured out the one thing that might actually hurt him. His bottom-line. Well done."

Anya blinked. She recalled, unwittingly, the look of absorption on her husband's face when she'd tried to slice him with her shoe.

He hadn't been hurt then, not really. But he'd stood there and let her hurt him anyway. As if he *deserved* it.

"Us scholarship kids have to be smarter than the rest of the trust fund babies."

"Well, you're the only one among the four of us who's getting a smart person degree, so kudos," Kit complimented her.

"What do you mean?" Anya demanded. "Drake's a Caltech student, isn't he? It says so in his bio."

"No, that would be me. I studied at Caltech," Kit admitted. "But I only scraped by because of my brother, Shiv. Drake was visiting faculty two years after we all graduated. But, as far as Lily tells me, Drake never even finished high school."

EIGHT

Drake never even finished high school.

Anya tried to wrap her head around those words, while inputting her final notes on The Green Fund project. This note involved invoking the opposite of the key man clause – wherein, if the principle investor, Drake, passed away the fund would be carried on by his heirs. It was her conclusion, a sort of fuck-you coda to the hours she'd spent researching government permissions, promising companies ripe for takeover, national GDP versus tax-payer contributions in seventeen economies.

And, to her utter elation, she'd learned more about how corporate structures were built in the last two weeks than she had in six years of dedicated schooling.

Sure, this deal was hypothetical and wildly ambitious in the extreme.

Because it made all the unsexy parts about making money - like accountability, climate change, utilizing labor over automation, give underprivileged people a chance at earning college degrees in seventeen different countries - important.

She'd learned enough over the last two weeks of working with Mili that Drake was the one billionaire on the planet who could actually do it. He'd put this plan into action, make it real.

Change the damn world *and* save it.

And, if not this project, he was definitely doing his bit anyway. With all the many anonymous and enormous donations he'd made. All from wealth he'd made off nothing except the power of his mind.

His un-fancy college degree'd mind.

It boggled *her* mind, the dichotomies of this man.

Tonight, she'd seen a side of him she'd never thought possible. With his family.

When he'd met her, he'd been a different man. A savior. A hauntingly sexy savior she'd been immeasurably glad to meet, even though *god,* it sucked to admit it to herself.

When she'd come to know him later, he'd been ruthless. Commanding. Intent on getting his own way.

But then, he'd taken care of her mother. Eaten the dinner she'd so graciously prepared, down cold.

He respected her space and privacy.

He…confounded her.

She'd thought it possible to hate him, to make him pay for taking her choices away, for manipulating her, by blowing up all his money. His hard-earned, well-deserved money. He'd not even batted an eyelid at it.

But, he'd been hurt when she'd asked him to not say her name.

He'd been quiet and withdrawn the whole time they'd been at the wedding.

Even though he claimed to have missed her. Enough to break his deal, the one thing he was known for, with her.

What was she to do? How was she to remain indifferent to him, angry with him when he actually accommodated her?

Also, didn't he deserve her anger?

Just because he was a beautiful man in some regards did not negate the monster in him. Did it?

Anya gripped her hair in frustration as soon as she hit send on the document to Mili's internal email.

This was not helping her. Nothing was.

But, maybe, she could get answers to a couple burning questions she had. And maybe, her logical brain mocked her, it was just an excuse for what she really wanted.

To see him.

~~~~~

Anya sprang from the bed. Shoving the laptop aside. She strode out of the spaciously appointed suite before she could second-guess herself into insanity.
~~~~~

Knocked on the door directly opposite hers, muttering to herself all the while. "What am I doing? What am I doing? What the hell am I *doing?*"

"Come in." He called out from the inside. "Door's open."

Anya took a deep breath and pushed the door to his suite open.

"Money's on the table, man. You guys take a long to deliver booze…" Drake trailed off, as he turned around from where he was sitting, at a table facing the city skyline. A stack of seven books, ranging from JD Barker to James Clear, were neatly post-it'd in bright neon colors.

A pool of light bathed half of him. Delineating his sharp, aquiline nose, the brilliance of one blue eye, reflected twice by the glasses perched on his nose.

His level gaze did not waver from her unpainted, totally stripped down face.

"Did you need something?" He was cordial but distant.

She knew it to be so, because she'd seen the heart of him. When she'd seen the joy on his face after being thoroughly dunked by Bret.

"I need answers."

He leaned into his swivel chair so it creaked under his weight. "What about?"

She noted, irrelevantly, that he'd not even changed clothes from the dinner at Lily's Cottage. His suit was a dark midnight blue with a light lilac shirt. No tie. His creased pants hugged powerful thighs half illuminated by the lamp on the table. His hands hung loosely between them, so she could see the sleeves weren't perfectly cuffed.

He was disheveled. Occupied.

And she was struck mute by the force of the thing eating her alive from the inside.

Desire.

Anya took a steadying breath and focused on the topic that first came to mind. "Did you not graduate high school?"

~ ~ ~ ~ ~ ~

He nodded, slowly. "Yeah. I dropped out at the start of my senior year. Hooked up with an offshore oil rig operation in the South. Near the Gulf Coast. It was the fastest way for me to make the kind of money I needed to make without having a fancy college education."

"So you could start your own company?"

He nodded, again. "Yes, that was the eventual plan."

"Wasn't it dangerous? I mean." She bit her lip as her thoughts swirled in unruly patterns. All of which had one dangerous motive.

I want you.

I want you.

I want you so much it frightens me.

"You know what I mean," she said, at last.

"It was dangerous. But all well-paying work is, isn't it?" He was so quiet. Cooperative, stripped down in a way she'd not believed possible. "It's one of the reasons the money doesn't bother me. Having it or losing it. Because it doesn't require me to hold down a valve with fire streaming off millions of gallons of combustible crude oil, designed to incinerate every inch of me."

She was being incinerated inch by inch. Standing there, looking down at him. So cool, so aloof. Like they were just having a normal, intimate conversation. Like this was okay.

"Weren't you afraid at all?"

He shook his head. "No. Being burnt to death did not frighten me."

Anya's breath stoppered, started again. Her eyes rounded. "Then what does?"

He gave her a crooked grin. "Having a dangerous woman wield a pointy shoe at me."

Anya gave a nervous chuckle. Ran a hand over her hair, disturbing it so it slid down from the sloppy bun she'd aimed for. "About that... all that? I'm sorry, Drake. I've been a total bitch and it's not like me so yeah. I'm sorry."

"Would you feel better if I accepted your apology?" He sat very still in the chair. The blue of his eyes extraordinarily bright against the glasses.

No. Kiss me till I feel better. Then fuck me till I don't.

"Yes," she said quickly. Thickly. "I'd feel much better."

"Apology accepted." He turned the chair around and looked at his laptop. "You have nothing to be sorry for, by the way. I have been told by everyone who's dear to me, that I deserve far worse."

"Why?" Anya wanted to move.

She was rooted to the spot. Mesmerized as she saw his shoulders bunch and move, his fingers flex against the laptop as he typed. The severely tailored lines of the suit jacket did not do any justice to him.

"Because." He turned around. Gave her a quixotic smile. One that did reach his beautiful eyes. "I ruined your life. Didn't I?"

She opened her mouth. To agree. To deny. She didn't know. All she knew was that a war was being fought within her. One in which she felt battered, ended.

Anya turned to the side, desperate to outrun her heated thoughts. Her gaze fell on the laptop screen.

She stopped dead as she processed what she saw. "What is that?"

He gave her a quizzical look. "That's my work. It's why I moved to Singapore in the first place. To establish this project."

"But that's The Verdant Fund project," she spoke slowly. Stupidly.

Drake nodded. "Yeah. Yeah it is." He removed his glasses, tucked them against the laptop.

She sucked in a pained breath because the movement was so ordinary. Just him removing his glasses; it struck her with the force of a physical blow.

What was happening to her?

"It's what the world needs from us right now. Accountability. I'm simply the first man of means to provide it."

She swallowed, her breath coming out in shallow gasps. While the war fought on, between her head, her heart, her body. "I worked on this project. Those are my notes."

He nodded, scratched the side of his head with one long finger. "I know. Mili told me."

"She didn't tell…Why are you using *my* notes?" She ended the question on a strangled note.

He shut the laptop down while the screen still flickered ghostly-white. "Because they are solid. Sensible. They put forth all my arguments in concise patterns. And, mostly because…because." He looked at his hands. "I had to use your magnificent brain, Anya."

Drake looked up, contrition written all over his hard face. "I'm sorry I shouldn't have…"

"Say my name," she whispered.

The war quietened down. Finished inside her. Because he never lied. And if he said her brain was magnificent then she believed him.

More, she trusted him.

And if she was going to be damned for it, then so be it.

His nostrils flared. His lips pursed. And his fingers clenched against the glasses. "I beg your pardon?"

"I said." She spoke clearly. "Say my name. It's okay to say my name."

Drake stood up, the chair skittering to a stop against the wall. He walked toward her, his footfall heavy and quiet against the plush carpeting. He still wore his shoes. So he was that scant quarter of an inch taller.

She craned her head up while he came to a stop right in front of her. Within touching distance. Kissing distance.

"Do you know what you're asking?" He breathed.

Anya nodded, her eyes enormous, as all the blood rushed to her pulse points. The one on her neck, on her wrists, the stiff points of her chest, the one between her legs that beat like a second heartbeat…

She put a hand to his chest. Right on the spot where she'd twisted the shoe heel in.

His lips parted, as if he couldn't speak.

"Anya."

Her knees weakened. She put the other hand on his shoulder.

He tilted his beautiful head down so she could smell him, sense him, feel only him. His arms and legs and chest, that fast-beating heart. His rampant arousal. It enervated her. Empowered her.

Drake buried his nose in her hair. "Anya," he breathed.

She turned her head a little to the side, just a little because he was so close she only had to move a fraction of an inch.

"Drake," she whispered.

Then Anya kissed him. Softly, so softly that he didn't respond at first. And she felt afraid. That maybe she'd misread everything between them. Maybe he didn't want her anymore.

He looked startled. His eyes flying open, incinerating her like the oil-rig fire might have done him. His lips parted. Padded and well-shaped and slightly wet from contact with hers.

Begging to be kissed.

So, she did it again.

And this time, he fixed his mouth on hers and kissed her back.

This time, there was no mistaking what was happening between them. What she'd asked for. What she wanted.

NINE

Anya strained up, almost on her toes so she could get closer to him. To those lips she'd not allowed herself to dream of. Preferring to work through her needs, her demented desires.

She nipped and sucked at his lips, burying her hands in his hair, so they feathered over her fingers. It was so undeniably arousing, she couldn't help rubbing her chest against him. Heat flooded, immediate and immense, between her thighs and all she'd done was kiss him once.

He opened his mouth allowing her access and she took what she wanted from him. Sweeping in, capturing his tongue with her own. Sucking on it aggressively until he hummed in his throat. He clutched her skull, the pressure bordering on the threshold of pain but she couldn't care.

She couldn't focus on it; she was dying from the taste of him.

Drake tried to snake his hands over her back, clad in a simple tee shirt with the arms cut off. But she was having none of it. This was her moment, her chance.

She pushed him blindly in the direction of the couch. And he let her lead. His steps dancing in tandem to hers, toeing off his shoes in hurried, frantic movements.

She stumbled over one and he simply lifted her in one arm, in a movement that left her breathless.

Anya moaned at the sexy action and they both landed on the backrest of the couch placed in the middle of the suite's salon.

His butt hit the satin-covered fabric of the couch and made a slushing sound as he rested his weight on it.

His legs bracketed her hips, her waist as she kissed him. Her arms around his neck, his jaw, his shoulders, needing to do this over and over again till she could stamp her imprint on his mouth, the corners of his lush lips, his tongue, the backs of his teeth.

Needing the same from him.

This time, when Drake snaked one hand under her oversize tee shirt, she didn't stop him. She just raised her arms up so he could lean closer, sucking strongly on her collarbone while he lifted it inch by torturous inch.

She trembled all over, when he brought her arms back down, twining his fingers around her knuckles, so her small palms enclosed his larger hands.

He was so absorbed in her hands, she could see the naked, yearning expression on his devastating face. An earthquake set off inside her, when he took both knuckles close to his mouth and kissed them softly. His bristle rustling against her tender skin.

Anya tugged her hands off and attacked his jacket, flinging it open, then trying to do the same with his fancy shirt with the tiny monogrammed studs. All the while, he kissed her, her cheeks, her jaw… her button-like nose.

She kissed him back. His lined forehead, the grooves near his eyes, her lips bestowing tiny benedictions. She kissed his eyes closed, his lashes feathering over her lips.

And finally, *finally,* she got his damned shirt open.

He flung it off, not bothering to check where it landed.

This time, when they kissed, there was no barrier of clothes, of lies or secrets between them. This time, her heart beat as fast and furious as his.

When he grabbed her back almost bringing her on him, she went willingly. His fingers were hard, almost bruising as they cruised over her skin, and she still couldn't stop kissing him.

It was she who almost climbed on him, wrapping one leg over his muscled thigh so her baby shorts rode up indecently high and bent his head back so she could kiss him deeper, harder. More.

He hummed in his throat again, followed by a rumble in his chest when she followed her lips down his jaw, down the strong column of his throat. Down to where his

Adam's apple bobbed with each gasping, straining breath he took.

Anya was untethered. Completely free in a way she'd not realized was possible. Because she was bound to him. Tied to him by whatever had exploded between them the second he'd touched her.

And, at the same time, she had power over him.

She understood this in some animal corner of her non-functioning brain. She rubbed and moved against him like a sinuous cat, basking in the warmth of sunlight, a mermaid sunning the rocks.

And he loved every second of it, filling his palms with her hips, squeezing them just a fraction too tight. Moving up her spine, vertebra by vertebra until he stopped midway and moved to the front. Closing his hand and lips around one aching, pouting nipple.

Drake sucked hard, pulling the tip between his teeth so she arched and shuddered and writhed against him.

Anya opened her lips wide, as she kissed his shoulder. The taste of his skin tangy with masculine musk. Essentially Drake. Then, she fastened her teeth on the spot she'd just kissed and sucked.

Drake growled, growing larger against the notch between her thighs.

He gripped her skull in one hand, hauled her back up and they just stared at each other. A little crazed with desire and hardly able to bear it.

~ ~ ~ ~

"Are you sure you want this, Anya?"

His voice was fathoms deeper than she'd ever heard it. His lips were cherry red from all her tender ministrations. There were marks on his cheeks, that hadn't been there a second ago.

His eyes blazed with infernal fire.

One that set off dozens of answering explosions inside her. In her womb, the tips of her wet breasts, the pulse point of her neck, her elbows, her knees, her very spine…

Drake squeezed her other breast in a large palm. Rubbing the nipple in tandem. As if he couldn't stop himself.

Anya touched the very spot on his chest where she'd dug the heel of her shoe in. There was a miniscule dent in his skin, a minor abrasion. Nothing to have actually hurt him. And he could have stopped her anytime he wanted. Instead he'd pressed the wound deeper.

Her lips parted on a silent sigh, as she stared at her handiwork. Riveted. Driven.

He captured her sweaty hand in his and he held it right there.

"Are you sure you want me, Anya?"

She couldn't speak. Because the things she wanted to say, damning and terrible things…*You're what I always wanted. I could be with you forever. My heart's beating out of my chest trying to get to you…* they made no sense.

They weren't true beyond this moment. Couldn't be.

Her vision hazed.

She sincerely hoped with what little common sense remained, they were untrue.

"Because you're what I wanted, Anya," he admitted.

Drake kissed her softly, sweetly on her cheek. Pushing one wayward curl behind the curve of her ear, caressing it delicately. Making her nerve endings dance all the way to her navel. Making her impossibly wet, impossibly deprived.

"I didn't know I wanted till I wanted you." His words were a shaky, heady whisper.

Anya swallowed a trembling breath at the enormity of his confession. At the hope and joy that danced in her along with the fire. The crazed need.

In answer, she reached between them and brought him closer by simply hooking one finger in his belt. She undid it, so it hung open between them.

"Come here," she ordered.

In answer, he braced her thighs between his waist, so she was forced to wrap her legs around his tapering hips. Kissed her, tonguing her so hard she literally saw stars explode behind her closed eyes.

His strong hands, gripped her butt, her thigh as he carried her over to the couch. Dropping into it with her in his arms. She landed with a little oomph, shook her hair off her face, her eyes.

Drake captured her jaw in one hand, as he stared at her. Consuming. Focused on her.

His other hand forayed into her shorts, stealing past her inner thighs. The kiss he gave her was sumptuous, delicious. So sweet she was drugged on it, when he used one finger inside her slicks folds.

Her eyes flew open at the sensation of him sucking on her tongue and pleasuring her where she needed it most. She arched into him, shuddering, undone.

Anya gripped his skull, sick with longing and pleasure, as she kissed him. Rubbing violently against his erection. The feel of him, thick and waiting, too much and yet not enough.

Almost as if she could stop the orgasm that was coming. That had been coming since she'd first kissed him. Stretching from her head to her heart, connecting to her womb.

He kissed her rapaciously, as starved for her taste as she was. Drinking the slick sounds of her as she tried to keep from climaxing.

"Let go, Anya." He muttered against her lips. "Let go for me."

And that was all it took. Just his harshly whispered words for the world to explode inside her. Glossy and slippery. She rode the wave, bending her back so he could suck at her breasts while he did unspeakable things to her deep inside. Crooking his fingers so far inside he hit something that lit her up.

She'd barely got her breath back, struggling to open her eyes, when he reversed their positions.

~ ~ ~ ~ ~

"Drake," she murmured drowsily.

He hooked one of her watery legs over his muscled shoulder and kissed the inside of her thigh.

"Drake, what…"

Drake grinned. An incorrigible little smile when he saw the skin bared by the Brazilian. "Nice." He drawled like the good ol' Midwestern cowboy he wasn't. "The better for me to taste."

She gripped his hand, the back of the couch, gouging her fingers on the fabric. Feeling it move exactly as her own skin, the insides of her was…against his wickedly erotic mouth. His tongue hot and abrasive, applying light pressure while he sucked on her clit, changing it up, moving up and down with intent, with pleasure. His hand on her stomach, to keep her in place.

Sounds escaped her, breathless and weak.

And the second orgasm hit her harder than the first, so she ground into the couch, against his lips, shamelessly asking for more. Which he gave.

When she finally managed to flip her eyes open, the world had somehow not ended. Her body was still intact. Bonelessly sprawled half on him and half on the couch.

"You…" Anya breathed.

"I'm dying," he growled. A golden god at her feet. Hungry and wanting, if the predatory look in his face, the hard cast on his cheeks was anything to go by.

She held leaden arms out to him, which was all the direction he needed.

~ ~ ~ ~ ~

He swept her into his arms again, and she was amazed at his strength. But he didn't go far. In fact, he just dropped her on the carpeted floor, taking care to protect her skull with his large palm.

Kissing her hungrily, sucking on her lips, moving down to her breasts, doing the same thing there. Then moving back to her lips.

Anya was so satiated that she could only offer herself to him. Her hands moving languidly over his back, over the ridged scars on his shoulders.

He was the one who kicked off his pants and belt, taking her shorts and simple white bikini panties with him. When he came back up, he spread her thighs wide and notched himself at her entrance, after quickly sheathing on a condom.

The feel of him inside her, too full to take in was more than she could bear…was all she wanted.

Anya had the fanciful thought that he was a dark, golden, looming specter she'd caught for the night.

She ran her hands leisurely down his chest, the little whorls of hair tickling the underside of her palms. She raised her knee so she had more balance while he sank into her, holding her gaze with his.

Drake captured her wrists in his own and placed them by her head, so she was naked, open, exposed like a sacrifice for him. She reveled in it.

He moved once. A long, slow, torturous threat.

Her breath caught and she shuddered.

He did it again. And again. Slow and heavenly, so it was a descent into orgasm. Thick, mindless, the only true thing on earth. His hands gripped her hard, harder as he thrust into her, as she wrapped one leg around his waist and took him in deeper.

It unchained something in him so he pounded into her, each slick move bringing him closer and closer to completion.

So the thing that had almost died of pleasure rose back up again in her. Swift. Breathtaking.

So, when she closed her eyes against the climax that overtook her, when she heard him growl something indescribable as he jerked hard against her in his own orgasm, almost collapsing on her, she still only saw his eyes.

Bluer than the sky at peak noon, and just as essential to her existence.

~ ~ ~ ~ ~

"My sister likes you," Drake murmured, eons later. The announcement was happy. Filled with a kind of wonder he'd have been appalled to know was within his capacity.

He ran a lazy hand down her hip and felt her corresponding shiver.

It filled something in him to know he could make her respond like that. That his touch affected her like that. He didn't know what to make of it so his brain decided to just enjoy it.

Anya stirred one sleepy eye open. She blew a lock of purple-tinted hair away from her sleep-flushed face.

He did the rest, taking the hair away and caressing the side of her jaw. She moved into that touch too, like a cat snuggling in.

It could become addictive, he realized. Touching Anya. His wife.

Where once the phrase had created disquiet and chaos in him, he now found…peace?

Drake blinked.

"Did you just wake me up to tell me your sister likes me?" Anya murmured sleepily.

She kissed the part of him closest to her, his bicep.

He moved closer, drawing her knee over his own. He wondered what she saw in him. His face which never revealed anything. He felt like it was flayed open around her. "Yes."

Anya smiled, looped one hand over his neck. And brought him so close, their noses brushed. "Flatterer."

He nipped at her lips just because they were there. "I feel better now."

"What about?"

"This is a much better first time, don't you think?"

Anya giggled. "First time?" Her eyes widened. "Oh, you mean…mine."

Drake nodded. "Yes, silk sheets. Huge bed. Good food and champagne. The whole works."

They were in his king-size bed together, the sheets in disarray from their activities over the last few hours.

Empty condom wrappers covered the surface of the marble nightstand, and an empty champagne bottle and two plates of half-eaten greasy fries done in truffle oil lay upturned near the towels they'd shed after a long, leisurely shower once they'd stumbled into the bedroom.

She blinked. Her eyes feline, golden. "Indeed," she murmured. Then she slitted a look at him. "Do you really care that much about how it was for me?"

He gave her a droll look. "Don't make me spank you, sweetheart. Of course, I care about how it was for you." Far more than he could understand…and it didn't worry him as much as it would have a day ago.

She squeezed his bicep. "You can spank me. Later," she murmured sleepily.

So satisfied, he had to grin.

"What's so funny?"

"You." Drake kissed her nose. "I exhausted you, didn't I?"

Anya's feline eyes flew open in indignation. She pushed him back on his chest and straddled him, pushing the boxers he wore further down his pelvis. "I'll show you exhausted, mister."

He ran a lazy hand down her thigh, skimming his shirt off her skin. Put his hands behind his head, so she could do what she willed with him. "Show me."

She leaned down and brushed noses with him, before biting it.

Drake howled, a grin kicking up the corners of his mouth. "That's unfair tactics."

"I'm smart. I don't play fair."

He speared his hand in her hair, held her skull in place so he could raise his head and give her a thorough kiss for that claim. When he was done, they were both breathing hard.

Anya placed both palms on his chest and squeezed. "I learned it from you."

~ ~ ~ ~ ~ ~

He swung her down in a swift motion that had her shrieking against him. The shriek ended in a sigh when he kissed her again. Soft, sweet. With a tenderness that took the edge of the rough need that had possessed him all through the night.

"You know what I was thinking?" He crooked a finger in her wet heat. It was convenient when there were no panties to rip off.

Her breath caught but she didn't let go of his gaze, her eyes limning with soft dewy desire. She dug her nails on his biceps. "What?"

"I don't have to go back just yet."

"Go back where?"

"Singapore. Home, you know," he reminded her.

"Home." The word, when it came from her, took on entirely new shapes. A definition he hadn't thought possible. But wanted more than anything now.

Because home had become the eyes of a woman with purple hair and gentle, questing, but surprisingly demanding hands.

"My home's in Little India. I share a bathroom with my mom and...*aah.*" She arched against him, rubbing her breasts against the hard line of his chest when he went deeper with two fingers than he had ever before.

His other hand smoothed her pelvis, hooked her navel in.

"Your home could be with me." He looked up from where he'd been about to kiss her belly button.

Anya opened lazy, loved eyes. And gave him a considering look. "Is that so?"

"Not immediately, of course," he rushed to reassure her. "We could take some time off. Travel around. I have meetings in LA, Philippines, and Cambodia. We could go to that private island in the Philippines, Boracay."

"I…" She bit her lip, conflict visible in every inch of her.

Drake kissed her stomach while the organ that beat blood into him shriveled just a little.

She doubted him. Even now. Even after last night and all that they'd done together. In several different positions. After he'd told her things he'd never told a living soul, she wasn't sure.

"It was just a thought, Anya. Don't worry about it, okay?"

She feathered a hand over his hair. Her elfin face was strangely pensive, even though she was so naked and responsive in his arms. A mysterious female with the universe hidden inside her. One he desperately wanted to access.

Because, for the first time, well…the first time since he'd looked across a crowded Bacchanalia party and seen her, he felt…quiet.

"Why do you want me to come with you?"

"Because I think your inputs would be valuable in these meetings," he replied promptly.

"Uh-huh."

Anya brought him up closer, so he kissed his way up her torso as he spoke. The valley of her breast, the vulnerable column of her jaw was nuzzled thoroughly.

"I'd rather have one of my best people. Person," he corrected lazily. "With me."

When he reached her lips, he found her absorbed in looking at him. As if she couldn't quite believe what she was seeing.

Or maybe that was just him. He couldn't believe he'd found this woman. With her brains and her brand of crazy, her guts and the tight, compact body which drove him wild.

"Why else, Drake?" She ran her hands up and down his arms as he braced himself over her.

"The perks of having you around are nice," he admitted.

She chuckled. "You *are* way better than my vibrator." She squeezed his butt and pulled him closer.

Drake framed her face with his hands. Unable to not touch her for more than a second. Amazed he'd allowed her to sleep for six hours when he'd stayed awake for the last two trying to talk himself out of what he was doing right now.

Coaxing her to be with him.

"I want you," he said quietly. "With me. And it is unsettling to want this for me but I want you with me. All the time."

Anya was quiet for a long moment. And he thought, he was sure she'd refuse. It wasn't a promise of any kind. And there was so much wrong with their...*deal.* But, the idea of staying away from her had no appeal anymore. So yeah, he did want her. With him.

Even if it scared the crap out of him.

She turned her lips to one side and kissed the side of his palm. "I have classes starting in four weeks. As long as I'm back for them, I'm yours."

Drake stared at her for a moment longer. The words were said with artless simplicity. He was sure she didn't mean it more than literally. And was freaked out by the idea of how much power she'd just given him with those two words.

"Drake?"

"Yeah." He gave her a brief kiss. "Okay." Another. "Good." He shucked off his boxers down his knees.

He raised her leg and drove into her, hearing the catch of her breath in the quiet roaring of his own heart. And this time, when the contentment and peace filled him when he loved her, when he took her past reason and flew into the sun with her, he was not afraid.

It felt right.

For the only time in his life.

TEN

Mili Iyer was a creature of habit. She'd trained herself to become a creature of habit because the alternative was to inhabit chaos and adults did not exactly live in chaos. Or thrive in them.

So, she woke up faithfully at the ungodly hour of six-thirty am, plugging in the fancy coffee machine Drake had gifted her last Christmas. She lived in a beautiful furnished pied-a-terre with a stunning view on Orchard Street, one of the most exclusive addresses in Singapore.

Her job did come with the best perks.

Mili did her meditation exercises before powering up the treadmill for her morning run. She checked her messages and phones (she had three), each of which had memos and documents and process statements to check.

Not to mention tasks which had to be delegated. She'd learned so much from working with Drake, the man had an uncanny talent for keeping every single aspect of a deal.

Whether it was seeding a company, funding a Series A with a group of like-minded people, investing in shares in a revolutionary tech or bidding for projects in Third World countries to do them better, cheaper, and with far more benefits than anyone realized.

And, though she did not have his mental capacity to recall every single detail of every single deal, she was insanely organized. She also had the rare capacity to delegate, ruthlessly and efficiently.

With no false modesty, she knew she'd risen to be Drake's executive aide at twenty-nine precisely because she could execute the nitty gritty of all the big picture deals he dreamed up and thought of, on the spur of the moment.

Work, holy and consuming work, was all her boss cared about.

Always.

If it did not benefit the bottom-line or whatever cause he was championing at the moment, he had no further use for it. The man only did holidays for Christmas because he wanted to spend time with his nephew.

It was the main reason Mili's schoolgirl crush on her hero had died a swift and merciful death. Any man who couldn't be bothered to be passionate and *real* was not worth her time or energy. Or, god forbid, her love.

She had a theory about why Drake was the way he was. And it most definitely had to do with an abused childhood followed by emotional and physical abandonment. None of which made him a functional adult and a bad bet, romantic styles.

Mili began her run, her mile-long legs easily keeping pace with the treadmill, even though it was set to the highest resistance setting. She finished swiping through her messages, and would have gotten off the thing when a new message pinged into her inbox.

She blinked and read it once. Then once again.

The buy on the bio-degradable satellite company is a go. I've signed the transfer papers. Going on vacation. Will check in intermittently. Keep the home fires burning and I trust you won't allow the stock market to crash on our heads. – Drake.

Mili shook her head. Because this had to be a REM dream.

Drake wasn't taking time off. From *work*. That was unheard of.

The second message was even more bizarre.

Instate my wife as a permanent employee in Fallahil Inc. Compensation decided by you on basis of skill assessment. – Regards, Drake.

She breathed hard, through the sweat and pain. The words going double in some places.

"What the fuck?"

Then the last message pinged into her inbox.

Remind me to give you a raise when I get back. For the purple hair. – Chef's kiss. Drake.

Mili lost her footing, stumbled off the treadmill, almost banging her head against the side of the machine. Her curse and laugh bounced off the walls of her apartment as she re-checked the message, while rubbing her bruised shin.

Well, hell had finally frozen over. Her perpetually dysfunctional, workaholic boss was on holiday.

And he wasn't inclined to fire her for helping Anya get her own back on him.

Mili smiled softly.

Maybe marrying Drake Fallahil wasn't akin to committing emotional suicide, after all.

～～～～

They ended up staying in Chicago for three more days. Sightseeing through the Art Institute, the famed 'Who Are You' sculpture and the Van Gogh moving art installation that she'd marveled at. He'd disliked the colors immensely but kept the heretic thought to himself.

Lily and Anya cooked dinner for the family one evening after they'd come back from seeing a Cubs pre-game session at Wrigley's. Anya was almost as excited as Bret at being seated in the private box and watching the proceedings.

From there, they'd flown to LA. He'd had meetings lined up on Sand Hill Road, half the distance between

San Francisco, Palo Alto and Los Angeles, with former investors, entrepreneurs he'd nurtured when he was first starting out. Anyone with half a conscience and a dollar to spare, actually.

Anya was so excited by the prospect of walking through the Maps of Stars route, Drake did not have the heart to keep her cooped up in his meetings. Although she'd generously offered to sit in with him.

In point of fact, her notes after his meetings concluded were invaluable to him.

So, they'd agreed on a compromise. She'd sightsee LA on her own, with Shane McRae by her side and he'd finish work as soon as he could and join her.

He had plans to drive them down to a small winery he owned in Napa rumored to produce an excellent Burgundy in the next two years, one of the few sentimental purchases he'd made over the years. Drake knew Anya would get a kick out of tasting wine owned by him.

"Are you sure you can't come with me, Drake?" Anya adjusted the angle of the hat she wore to keep the sun out of her face in the free-standing mirror in his Malibu pad.

It was a beautiful private bungalow with private access to the beach, was built into a mountain-side bluff.

It was the first major investment he'd made after he joined the Three Comma Club. It had cost him upwards of seven figures but was totally worth it, for the view alone.

Especially now, Drake thought with contentment.

"I know watching the stars in the daytime is your idea of fun. But I will be bored out of my skull."

"I'm going to visit the Griffith Observatory. It's supposed to be pretty and informative." Anya gave him a mock-glare. She wore high-waist jeans and a layered, off the shoulder tee that hugged every exquisite inch of her. Her ridiculous hair was left open to curl wildly around her lovely face.

He shrugged. "Not my idea of fun or informative. What's the point in counting stars, babe?"

"There's no point…" She threw her hands up. "Never mind. I'll see you after?"

Anya dropped down to give him a quick kiss. He turned it into a full-fledged exploration of her tongue, the insides of her mouth. Turning hard in an instant too.

"Do you really have to go?" Drake murmured, as he nosed his way down her neck. "I could cancel my meeting. Who cares about saving the world…" He snuck his hand up her shirt. Squeezed her nipple. "This is more important."

Anya batted his hand away, laughing into his mouth. "You're disturbing my hat, babe. I set it on a jaunty angle."

He flopped back on the bed. "It's perfect."

Anya smiled sweetly at him. "Thank you, kind sir. Now go save the world. Will you?"

~~~~~
~~~~~

He was still thinking about her words as his meeting concluded, the easy faith she displayed in him when she shared so generously of herself with him. Her body. Her mind. He didn't know which fascinated him anymore – the soft heat of her or the razor sharpness of her brain.

All he knew was, he was fascinated by his wife. Period.

The woman he was legally bound to but who'd made no claims on him otherwise.

Anya was the one person in his orbit who'd never asked anything for herself. In fact, she never asked for anything at all.

She'd been beyond pleased and cooked him dinner when he'd helped with her mother's surgery. And she was equally excited and cooked him dinner in the Malibu pad's sterling kitchen, *naked* when Mili had sent her employment contract over for approval. It wasn't something she'd angled for.

She deserved it.

Anya was more interested in catching musicals and having four different kinds of acai ice-cream than she was in blowing up his money on Rodeo Drive. She could spend hours watching the stars up in Griffith Observatory instead of seeing Hollywood royalty drive by in Bel Air.

And she never really asked anything of him. Not his time. Not his resources. Not even his desire.

No, he was the one who turned to her, grabbing her wherever and whenever the mood struck him.

It all fascinated him. And if he had anyone to confide the puzzle of her with, he would have.

His phone rang. And he answered it without bothering to check for caller ID, because only Mili and Anya had access to this number. And Mili knew better than to call him when he'd given explicit instructions not to.

"Missing me?" He sounded besotted, Drake realized even as he said the words.

"Should I be, Drake?" Aster's dulcet tones floated through the phone.

~~~~~

His good mood evaporated into ashes. "Aster? What the fuck do you want?"

"To talk to you, Fallahil. Warn you actually."

"Warn me? What about?"

"Ajay and Jay Runwal have discovered that your people have been looking into their affairs. I came to know of it because their dad plays golf with mine every month. Ajay's pissed with you, Drake," Aster said softly. "He thinks you're friends."

"How on earth did he get that idea?" Drake asked blankly.

"Maybe because you attended his Bacchanalia? Fucked a girl there and broke the nose of one of his security team?" Aster asked dryly.

"What's that got to do with anything, Aster?"
~~~~~

"Nothing. I know you think you're untouchable. And maybe you are," she conceded reluctantly. "Ajay Runwal, particularly, does have more skeletons than you do."

"I bet he does. Sha…My people haven't even finished compiling it. And besides," Drake said idly, thinking three moves ahead as always. "I'm thinking of going into business with him. We're still looking for ground to break for the new office complex."

"Of course, you are."

"So maybe," he murmured. "I can rely on you to pass this message back to him? When I get back to Singapore we could get together and hash the details out."

"Sure," Aster said doubtfully. "I'll find a way to get the message to Ajay. But, Drake. Be careful. Ajay didn't get to where he was by playing nice."

"You're concerned about me, Aster," Drake drawled. "How touching."

"Fuck you too, Drake," she said cheerfully. "I'm only calling because I owe you for my job with Chan Holdings. I'm rooting for Ajay to fleece you dry. See you never, Fallahil."

Drake ended the call more thoughtfully and typed out a message to Shane. Asking him to expedite his findings with the Runwals.

Because, in the sexual haze he was living in, he'd finally remembered the very first reason he was fascinated with Anya.

She'd broken into the Runwals' server room. And he'd never figured out why.

The time had come, Drake ruminated, to get some answers from his wife.

The phone pinged again. He swiped it open.

It was a picture message from Anya. She was posing against the Observatory's panorama. Her message said, *Wish you were here.*

Drake texted back without thought. Pressing a button on his fancy watch that would get his car and driver to the entrance of the Bay Area's fanciest restaurant, a freaking burger joint.

As you wish.

ELEVEN

"Honeymoon suits you, *beta*. Three weeks away from all responsibility and you've even put on a little weight." Swati observed affectionately. She brushed a hand over Anya's hair as they prepared the dough for the *aloo parathas* Ishqi had insisted on for lunch.

And her mother, being her mother, was indulging Ishqi's every whim.

Anya stuffed the mashed and marinated spicy potatoes into the rolled dough ball before pressing it back. Like rolling a dumpling, but without the fancy pouching. She said nothing to the off-hand comment, which was a little offensive, when you really thought about it.

"Where is my sister dear?" Anya asked Swati.

Swati brushed sticky hair off her forehead and wrinkled her nose. "Out somewhere. You know she doesn't like to stay home. Unless she's eating. Or sleeping."

"Don't you think being in prison should have changed her the slightest bit? Made her more…mindful of your feelings, mama?" Anya spoke quietly, knowing she was treading on eggshells.

"She's Ishqi. She's not going to change that easily, you know." Swati shook her head immediately. Pivoted on one hip and took the ball Anya had rolled, swiftly patting it on the floured surface and rolling it into a round shape with an old-fashioned *belan*, a rolling pin.

Anya marveled at her mom's ease of movement in the time she'd been away.

Apparently, Swati had ditched the walker as soon as she came home and thrown herself into the physical rehab. As a result, she was now able to stand for hours on end without wincing in any pain. And her gait was as straight as it had never been.

Modern medicine was miraculous indeed.

"Still." Anya popped some mashed potato in her mouth. It was delicious, spiced to perfection with the exact amount of coriander garnish to not overwhelm the potatoes. "She has to learn to be a little more responsible for her own good."

Swati sighed. Placed the loaded *paratha* on the hot pan. It sizzled against the butter already gently simmering on the pan. "She's young still, *beta*. She will learn."

"She's older than me, Mom," Anya said softly. "God knows I learned responsibility when I was in diapers."

Swati looked startled. "I never asked you to be responsible for me and Ishqi, Anya. Don't make this out to be my fault."

Anya shook her head. "I'm not blaming anyone. I think I am a dedicated workhorse in general. But it never helped that Ishqi was given all the freedom to hang out and have fun with friends while I was stuck helping you with cooking."

"I thought you liked helping me, Anya." Tears filled Swati's eyes. "Why didn't you say anything, then?"

Anya stopped rolling the *parathas*. Leveled a condemning gaze on her mom. This conversation was a lifetime coming and she felt ready to have it now. Three weeks in Drake's unassuming company had given her perspective into her own situation.

"I felt like I had no choice, mama. You were alone in a strange country, trying to make ends meet. Struggling with my wayward sister. You didn't need me to throw tantrums too."

"But you were my child," Swati protested loudly. "All you needed to do was tell me you didn't want to help me with chores. I'd have managed by myself."

"I was," Anya agreed. "I was the dutiful, responsible child. Always doing the right thing. Helping you and Ishqi out whenever you need me. And now you don't, do you?" Anya said softly. "You don't need me anymore."

Swati sighed. Turned the paratha on the pan. "Is that such a bad thing, Anya? Me not needing you? For the first time in years, I'm not in pain. I can move, walk, cook."

She indicated the stove. "I'm strong. I feel…alive. Is it so wrong to want that for me, *beta*?"

Anya shook her head. "No, mama. I want this for you. I've always wanted you to be free."

"And it's not like you need me, Anya. Like I'm a part of your decisions," her mom continued, bewildered. Slightly accusing. "I didn't even know you were seeing Drake when you told me you were marrying him. You found him all on your own, didn't you?"

"Yes," Anya whispered, as a thick ball of tears lodged in her chest. "I found him alright."

"So it all worked out alright, in the end, right? You have Drake and I have myself and Ishqi will find what she wants too, *beta*." Swati reached over and squeezed Anya's shoulder. She left a dusting of flour on her black shirt. "I didn't know you felt so badly about being with me. Maybe I should have allowed you to move out when you got into NUS."

"Don't be silly. We couldn't afford it. It is all okay now. And besides." Anya tossed the rolled ball into her mom's waiting hands. "Where else could I find the world's greasiest *parathas* in the world at one am?"

Swati smiled, mollified. Back to her cheerful self with those placating words that Anya, to her credit, half-meant.

When they were done, Swati sat down to eagerly see the million pictures Anya had taken of the many places they'd visited. The virgin beach in Sector 14 on Boracay Island in the Philippines where one needed police permission to enter. The Shinto shrine in Tokyo and the floating flower market in Laos.

The Griffith Observatory pictures with Drake.

She dutifully recounted the specialties of each place they'd visited, and her mom was suitably impressed. She was touched too because Drake had specifically ordered Anya to buy souvenirs for Mili and Swati from each place they'd visited.

It was such a sweet unexpected gesture from him she'd complied without demur.

Anya demolished her fair share of the parathas, boxed a few up for leftovers and took the MRT back to Marina Bay station. Mindful of her mom's comment about her weight, she decided to walk the rest of the way to the Trident.

~ ~ ~ ~ ~ ~

She was still thinking about the many unpredictable moods of the man she'd shared the most magical of summers with, during her trek through the lush paradise off Gardens by the Bay.

Drake was playful, amusing, and insanely brilliant while making skewering observations about the people they'd meet on the way. More than that, he was *nice* to her. Not in the way of opening doors or being generally chivalrous, but he complimented her in the exact way she needed.

Her brain, for one. When he took her notes into serious consideration as he built the many branches and sub-strata of The Verdant Fund, the world over.

Her goofy sense of humor when they shared a late night comedy show together.

Drake was a fanatic for health so he woke up at ungodly hours, wherever they were and punished himself on fancy gym equipment.

She couldn't complain because it gave him the strength and vitality of a much-younger man and she took full advantage of his sweaty self every time he came to their hotel suite and jumped him.

He'd charmed her when he'd come to Griffith Observatory and spent an hour wandering aimlessly, trailing behind her when she'd asked him. He'd done it again and again as they jetted around the world in his private jet, no Shane McRae around to guard them.

Booking exotic treks and tours in the places they visited. Inviting her to sit in on meetings with the heads of Fortune 500 companies and, in the case of Cambodia, the entire freaking nation.

She was a green, twenty-four year-old MBA student. She shouldn't have the power to tell the leader of a country how to save energy and provide a plan for jobs creation which did not harm the environment.

That kind of blind trust, him relying on her acumen, that was heady. Terrifying.

Precious.

And then, of course, there were his kisses. Each time tinged with a small amount of desperation, because he never not gripped her skull, diving his fingers in between her hair to kiss her.

When he trapped her in an elevator while a CEO waited for them and made her come with his mouth alone.

When he helped brush her hair before her elaborate hair baths. His normally blazing eyes soft as a dewdrop when he sifted the strands of her hair between his fingers to cause minimal damage.

Something had shifted inside of her, bit by bit, as if all the walls she'd built around herself, the things she'd had to do in order to survive were now a distant memory.

Where this, this *life* she was building and living with this man was more real than they'd ever been.

As if that was right.

Anya closed her eyes as she let herself into the penthouse she now shared home. The truth hitting her with all the force of a lightning bolt.

"God, I'm so in love with him."

~~~~~
~~~~~

She pressed a fist against her tumbling stomach at the quietly horrified words. Her normally contained thoughts careened into free-fall.

This wouldn't do. This wouldn't do at all. They were playing out a charade, a dream sequence from a life neither of them were really ready for. They weren't *married* for real because that required commitment and feelings and *declarations*.

I want you with me.

Anya desperately shook her head. That was not a declaration of anything. That was fact. He wanted her. Constantly. Always. Every single night.

So did she.

That did not mean anything, apart from them being unattached adults with a healthy sex drive.

So what if their silences were compatible with each other? As if she knew when he needed time and space to work out a complex issue? So what if their tastes were more alike than even she had anticipated – from food to music to pastimes?

So what, if every time he touched her she wanted to fall apart at his feet? Content, safe in the knowledge he'd catch her. He'd never let anything happen to her that she didn't choose for herself.

A sob ripped the air.

Anya closed her eyes even as the ocean roared in her ears. Like the beat of her own heart. The drive of her own pulse. An onslaught of feelings, too many of them, she couldn't contain them anymore.

And each of those feelings belonged to him.

As did her heart.

Anya let out a miserable sigh.

You foolish girl! How could you?

She rubbed at the ache under her breast. One that had built and built over the last few weeks, since the first second she'd turned around and seen his wicked eyes, if she was being honest with herself. Those eyes that had become dearer to her than anything in the world.

If this was love she didn't want it. It hurt.

Anya took another breath, stronger than the one before.

She was a smart, sensible, competent woman. She knew the deal here. Share his bed, his home, his life for the duration of the arrangement.

They'd not talked about what would happen when the clock wound down on their arranged marriage. But she knew. Because it was the most obvious thing in the world.

They'd go their separate ways.

And she was fine with it, she told herself. She was totally fine with it.

"This sucks." The words energized her into action.

Anya's best strength was how she utilized her brain. So she decided to utilize it towards not loving Drake. It was the best course of action.

To this end, she drew herself a lush, fragrant bath in the decadent bathroom. Stripped down, bundling her hair up so the curls wouldn't get wet. Put on some pulse-pounding rock and began talking herself out of it.

~ ~ ~ ~ ~

It was how, Drake found her forty-five minutes later.

Anya opened her tired eyes, tears shoved down to a deep dark place for now.

And there he stood. The man who haunted her dreams while somehow making them come true.

He wore another one of his suits. This one in severe black, with a black shirt, and an open jacket open. His tie and pocket square was a slash of devil-red against the funeral black. And his eyes were thoughtful when they landed on her.

"Hey, you. I wasn't expecting you home for an hour more," she said. "Mama sent *aloo parathas* when I went to visit her. So dinner's sorted."

He held up one elegantly muscled hand. A fine chain dangled down from it. An impressive tear-drop sapphire tugged the chain toward the ground. "What was this doing in a pawn shop off Orchard, Anya?"

She sat up a little straighter. "I… How did you find it?" She instantly made it about him.

"My security team found it when they were looking into your movements."

"I see." Anya should have felt offended at the gross invasion of her privacy.

But, the truth was, Drake was a supremely important man and, by associating with him, she'd become slightly important too. She wasn't surprised Shane McRae was digging into her background.

It was just a matter of time before Drake knew about Ishqi. Through someone else… Anya didn't want that anymore. She didn't want to keep anything from him anymore.

Drake walked, no, loped towards her. His gait predatory, his eyes completely unreadable. Even his hair did not move with each step he took towards her. When he reached her, he knelt down on the dais, his pristine trousers catching the wet.

"Will you promise to not lie to me, Anya?" He touched her arm. So gently, in entreaty.

"That's your thing," she whispered. "Not mine."

"Okay." He looped the chain around her neck and pulled it forward, bringing her with it.

His eyes were so soft, non-judgmental. The hard cast was gone from his face and in its place was her lover, her love. The man who'd given her more than she'd ever dared to dream.

Anya's heart broke clean in two. Two fat tears rolled down her cheeks and she whispered, "I have an older sister. I pawned this to get her a good lawyer so he could get her out of jail."

"Is she a troublemaker like you?" He kissed her nose.

"Why aren't you mad at me?" She demanded angrily.

The water sloshed between them. The flower petals she'd scattered around the surface splattering on his shirt. His jacket. He didn't even look down to check on them, his eyes steady on her defiant face.

"I hocked your stuff to keep my criminal sister out of prison. She's a hacker by the way," Anya fairly bit off the confession. "She does all sorts of things on the dark web."

"Uh-hmm?" Drake kissed her streaming cheek. "Is she any good?"

"She's very good. Why she was arrested in the first place. She'd done some shady stuff for Ajay Runwal, looked into some tenders for project bids. He didn't want to pay her for it. So he had her thrown in jail over a trumped charge."

His eyes filmed over into darkness. "That motherfucking bastard."

She nodded. "It's why I was there at the Runwals, that night we met. I wanted to find proof of Ajay's misdeeds. But I couldn't..."

"Yeah, we know how that turned out." He trailed his nose, his lips over her cheeks. "Do you know, you smell like a daisy?"

Anya leaned back and tried to shrug off his hold. "Did you hear me, Drake? I am a liar and a thief and not a very good one at that."

She sniffed loudly, even as the twin knowledge of her perfidy and her love crashed into her like a meteor hitting earth. Causing instant and total devastation.

"You're a good sister is what you are, Anya." Drake spoke quietly, his arms tight around her. An unbreakable band. A solid, safe sanctuary. "I don't blame you for anything you've done. You know that, don't you?"

"Why not?" She asked bitterly. "I do. I hate myself. Why shouldn't you?"

He shook his head, and gave her a look of utter trust. "I don't. I couldn't hate you if I tried."

A huge sob tumbled out of her. She clapped a hand over her mouth, horrified at the sound. At what it meant.

Drake leaned in further, his chest getting wet. Kissed her forehead. The gentlest of benedictions. "I could never hate you, Anya."

But you don't love me.

She covered her eyes with her hands as tears streamed uselessly down her cheeks and Drake held her in the safe haven of his embrace.

TWELVE

A little while later, Drake leaned into Anya, while she lazily washed his back. He looked up at the skylight, saw a gentle rain was pattering on the glass tiles. It added to the ethereal romance of this moment.

He contrasted it with the time he'd found Aster here. Perfect, gorgeous Aster. Everything a man, even him, had once upon a time wanted. Aster wouldn't be caught dead with purple hair streaming every which way, her eyes rimmed red from incessant crying.

Aster wouldn't know how to be this honest, this authentic.

Maybe that was why he'd not been tempted by the thought of marrying her. Share a bed, a life, his innermost self with her. Because she'd never reciprocate. She didn't know how to.

Something heavy, almost knife-like, twisted inside his chest, when he recalled the depthless sorrow in Anya, when she'd come apart in his arms. Her silent crying stabbing him, even now. Making him feel something he'd not felt in a long, long time.

Powerless.

"Hey." She kissed his right shoulder. A slight fairy perched behind him. "You're supposed to relax in a bath. Not clench your fists." She kissed his other shoulder. "Loosen up, sweetie."

Drake gave her a sideways glance. "Did you just call me sweetie?"

"Yes. It's cuter than honey but not as dignified as darling."

She kissed his back again. Right near, but not at the scar that bisected his shoulder blades. In all the times, she'd touched him freely, over and over again. She'd never touched those scars. Shying clear of them.

As if she possessed some instinct that told her to steer away from them.

He cracked a half-hearted smile. "Is that so?"

She nodded and some of her wild, wonderful hair slipped and touched the scar.

He'd lost a lot of sensation there, the raised skin having become numb over the years. But tonight, he felt the silken dragging of her hair. Dragging him closer to the edge of some abyss after which there was nothing but...

Falling.

He dragged her hands forward so she embraced him with arms and legs, her thighs cradling his sides. A slight fairy, still a fairy who held him straight and true. Safe.

"My father would beat me. As a child," Drake began slowly. In a low voice. "I think it was my earliest memory of him. That he'd beat me. Whaling into me with a belt. With a stick. Whatever was handy after he'd lit into the Kentucky Moonshine. My mother never did a thing to stop him. But she was so slight he'd have killed her with one backhand so it was a good thing she didn't."

He felt more than heard her outraged breath.

"Then, my sister, Lily, was born. And our mom, god bless her soul, passed away. I became responsible for her. She was just this…" His hands sloshed in the water. As he measured the weight of the baby Lily had been. "This tiny thing. Weighed next to nothing. Had the bluest eyes and sunniest head of hair I'd ever seen on a person. I'm not a religious person but I was convinced she was…"

His voice broke. "Heaven-sent."

Anya held him tighter, her arms going around him. She gave him the gift of her silence, her undivided attention. Even her breathing quietened down.

"I swore to myself, no one would ever touch Lily. Not the monster who raised me or the one who bore her. I did my best to protect her."

"You took your dad's anger on yourself," she concluded. "You let him punish you."

He shook his head. "I protected her. That's all. Whatever it took. All of this…" He waved his hand around the bathroom he'd never used for more than ten minutes. The perfect symbol of the life he'd built for himself.

Top of the world. Perfect. Untouchable.

"That's what it is. So we're safe. Lily and I. And Bret."

"But, who protected you, Drake?"

Drake closed his eyes. As years and years of unfed fear and spewing rage mixed inside his blood. Threatened to turn into molten fire. Unleashing the monster inside him, making him what he was always afraid, he'd anyway become.

His father.

"I don't need protecting, Anya," he denied instantly. "I never did."

"Oh, love." She kissed his scar then. A deep, enervating press of soft lips on the ugliest part of him. The weakest.

He grabbed her hands in hard fingers, intent on stopping her.

But she didn't stop. She allowed him to crush her fingers while she kissed up and down both his scars. The measure of his shame, the symbol of the helpless, innocent, confused child he'd been.

"Stop it, Anya," he said.

But she didn't stop. She kissed the scars over and over again, until the skin there tingled in reaction. In becoming alive again.

Drake stretched his shoulders, took a deep shuddering breath. One that tore out of his very gut. He released it in a great heave. And, in that moment, felt the weight of the scars he carried on his body float away. Banished under the gentle, healing power of her kiss.

This young woman who had the promise of her whole life in front of her. Brilliant. And endless. And exciting.

Drake's heart stopped. He could feel it thud down for a single microsecond.

Because her kisses had turned him back into a man. The stone heart of him was melting. Giving way, crumbling into nothing because she was here. She'd heard the whole damning story, all of his stories, and she was still here.

She was his.

And he…

Drake stared unseeing into the white petals of the daisies floating around them. Scenting the bathroom and his body and his very soul with the desire to be something he'd never thought to be.

Better.

Worthy.

~~~~~

"Turn around," Anya ordered. A gentle command.

He was powerless to resist her.
~~~~~

He maneuvered around the tub, water sloshing over his clothes carelessly tossed at the dais. Some of the daisies floated down too, fragile flowers bruised into nothing.

Drake picked one up and tucked it into Anya's wild hair. He framed her cheeks in his hands. And understood he might just be holding his absolution in his palms.

"Beautiful," he murmured.

Anya smiled tremulously. Clutching at his wrists with her own desperate hands. "Don't lie. It's the one thing you never do."

"You." He leaned forward, bringing them as close as it was possible to be, thighs entwined, supporting her back on his knees so his aching arousal nudged at her entrance. "Are." He kissed her hot ear, sucked the soft lobe into his mouth and felt the breath catch in her throat. "Beautiful."

She caught his hands in hers, kissed the feather-dusted knuckles. Tears shimmered in her gilded eyes, the hundreds of artificial candles giving her more mystery and poignancy than he could bear.

Every expression, each look she'd ever given him etched on his heart in that moment.

From scorn. To disdain. To anger. To fear. To arousal. And now this…tenderness. Warmth. Companionship.

"You're beautiful." Anya brought his lips closer to hers. "You're the most beautiful thing in the world, aren't you?"

The kiss they shared was soft, merciful. It wasn't the violent mating of tongues and teeth and lips he often indulged with her, as if he was starving and had to gulp her taste down in seconds before he lost it forever.

Tonight, it wasn't fast. It wasn't violent.

It was slow. Musical.

Heaven-sent.

When she angled her mouth just so, so he could suck on her tongue. When she kissed the taut line of his jaw and he couldn't help the grunt that escaped him as her delicate pink tongue toyed with his skin.

When she made him rise and went down on her knees, water streaming everywhere around them. The last of the purple streamed in rivulets down her hair, so she really did look like an enchanting fairy, with wild hair and the world's lushest mouth and breasts.

"Anya," he breathed because he could see the intent in her amber eyes.

"You're my most beautiful thing," she whispered.

Then she took his aching length in her mouth and Drake clenched his fists so tight against his palms the nails dug into his skin. She took one of his hands and wrapped it around her hair, so he could hold it back and away from her face. All the while moving her lips up and down him.

Drake threw his head back, unsure if his cock, his knees, his insides could take the onslaught.

By some magic, but mostly by clever design, the rain shower over the bathtub burst into life. As if the heavens themselves had opened up for this moment. The water sluiced down his back, his shoulders, washing away the last of the shame and helplessness he'd always associated with his scars. The boy he'd been.

When Anya looked up from her absorbing task, his smile was as tremulous, as unsure as if he was a newborn. Rising in her arms. Her lips. The life that had exploded between them.

She drank of the shower. It fell on her parted lips.

And he lost what was left of his mind as he saw the goddess kneeling at his feet. Brown-tipped breasts, tanned golden skin, ropes of hair that held him captive even though he was the one holding her. Her tawny eyes holding and promising the secrets of a star being born.

"You'll drown."

"You won't let me." She kissed the underside of his erection.

Drake felt a hot trickle on his cheek. He touched it. It felt different from the perfectly-heated shower water.

Was he crying? He never cried.

Anya took him further down her throat, her hand moving up and down in tandem with her lips.

His knees unbalanced, his heart threatened to leap out of his chest and straight out to the sky. To join the rain coming down from the heavens.

Drake roughly jerked himself out of her busy fingers. Sank to his knees next to her, wrapping her in his embrace so the water didn't hit her directly in the eye. Stinging her tender skin with needle-like pricks.

"What?"

Drake shook his head, the water streaming around him. Above him. From inside him.

"Thank you," he whispered rustily. In the warm shell of her ear. "Thank you for this gift."

Anya leaned back, blinking water from her eyes. "I didn't finish."

"No." he agreed. Hoisting her above him so she was half out of the tub. She squealed and clutched at his shoulder, his neck for balance. He sucked the water right out of her pert breast.

Anya sighed, slumping over him, as if her head was too heavy to support her.

"Put your legs around my waist," he said softly.

She did as he asked. Water sloshed everywhere, but more water took its place. Like the feelings being displaced inside him, reforming and refilling into something else. Something new and terrifying.

And awesome.

She framed his face between her trembling hands. Kissed him deeply, as if he *was* the most beautiful thing in the world. He could feel her crying, the sobs shaking her slender shoulders, turning her chest cavity concave.

He tried to brush them off with thick, stubby thumbs. But the damned things filled his eyes too. Wanting to come down.

So he did the next best thing.

He made love to her, with the sound of the rain and the water and the combined sounds of their tearing sobs, panting breaths. He made love to her because that is what this was. The feeling inside him.

Cleansing all the hurts, soothing all the wounds, healing all the scars.

This was why he'd come home today. When the necklace resurfaced. Why he wasn't angry with her for her revelations. Why he'd *revealed* her the truth of him.

Because she was his home. His heart. The love he'd never thought to find because he knew he wasn't capable of it.

And Drake knew, when he saw her close her eyes, her body bowed against the climax that wrung her inside out, although she was safe, safe in his arms.

He knew even when he followed her, the explosion setting off a cavalcade of reactions in him. So much so that he was blinded by the speed and tension of it.

He knew, he'd never get to keep her. Not when he'd been such a bastard and manipulated her into marrying him. When he'd done the absolute worst thing and taken away her choice to be with him.

To reject him.

Anya was too good, too fine for him.

She was noble and decent and glorious in her defiance. She'd taken on the devil of the business world and won.

She didn't even know that he was lost to her. And always would be.

THIRTEEN

"Walking with you is no fun," Anya complained a few days later.

Drake gave her a distracted glance when she tugged at his elbow, indicating he should slow down. "Hmmm? What did you say, sweetheart?"

Anya shook her head. A pleased light entered her golden eyes. "Never mind what I said. What are you obsessed with right now?"

"I'm not..." He automatically protested.

"Liar." Anya went on her toes and gave him a quick kiss.

He kissed her back, pressing his lips to hers, almost as if he could hold her there with the force of his lips. But, the more he thought about it, the more he was coming to a stunning conclusion.

He couldn't force her to stay with him anymore.

It wasn't right. It wasn't *fair* to her.

It might be all sorts of legal but legal had no place in the scheme of things anymore.

Drake was beginning to suspect, in those quiet moments when he woke up and saw Anya sleeping deeply beside him, her back curved away but into him, that legal had never had any place in the scheme of things between them.

And every time he woke up he was struck by the odd fear that his time with her was running out.

Not because they'd signed some damned contract. But because he was going to screw it up badly with her. He would have no choice but to.

After all, what did he know about being a good partner? A supportive one?

Anya winked at him, breaking his reverie. "I was kidding. I know you don't lie, Drake."

He gave her a smile that felt strained to him. "I know that. I know that you know me."

But do you like the parts of me you know? Can you accept them and me? Can you lov...

"So, this is how you keep fit? You just walk everywhere at odd hours?" Anya resumed walking, tucking her arm through his.

He looked down as she gazed up at the luxurious emerald world of the Gardens by the Bay they were visiting. All around them, soft music chimed and tinkled as if the heavens themselves approved of the three hundred feet tall trees shooting up to the sky. Lit up in soft, rechargeable solar tea lights in a myriad of colors.

Since it was almost closing time, there were hardly any visitors over the walkways and catwalks built between the trees.

Anya breathed deep, her translucent lids closed, as if to inhale the scents of the gardens inside her.

Drake felt familiar heat snake through him as the movement did interesting things to her chest. "Something like that," he murmured.

Then, before he could talk himself out of it, "Would you like to go out with me?" he asked restlessly.

Anya opened her eyes. Gave him a quizzical smile. "I don't understand."

"What's to understand?" He untucked her hand from his. Gripped it between both of his. Gripped also by a sudden inspiration which seemed like the perfect solution to his silly misgivings. "I want to take you out. On a date. You know. Champagne. Candles. Conversation. Anywhere in the world. Just say the word and we can go."

He could feel her entire being curve into him with each word he said. Her spine melted, she stepped closer to him, her face softening so it was wreathed in a swoony smile, her eyes glowing with sunshine and happiness by the time he was done.

Yes, this was the right decision. Date her. Woo her. Give her some kind of a choice so he didn't feel like…

"I didn't think we had time to goof off from work, considering you still haven't found a property for the

Singapore office complex, sweetie." She was ever the practical one. "After all, Verdant is not just your baby. She's mine too."

Drake's breath contracted at the idea of actually doing it…having Anya's belly swell with his child if they were granted that miracle. He was freaked out by how right it seemed. *What the hell had he become?*

"We're finalizing a property today for the office complex. As for work, I'm your boss, aren't I?" he challenged her. "I can afford to be…" He bent down and kissed the side of her neck. "Generous. Lazy."

"Unlike you?" Anya tugged his head back and beamed at him. "I love it."

"Then it's settled. We're going out tonight."

Anya shrugged. "How about we postpone this most romantic of dates for the weekend and I just order us some *nasi goreng* noodles for dinner tonight?" She kissed his cheek and nuzzled her nose against his jaw. "We can definitely have champagne with it, though."

Drake stopped walking. "Don't you…"

"Don't I what?"

"How come you've never had a serious relationship ever, Anya?" He asked quietly, driven by a curiosity beginning to eat him alive.

~~~~~~

He'd found the bare bones of her private life in a folder prepared by Rowan and his men but he couldn't believe it till he'd heard it from her own lips.
~~~~~~

She shrugged. "Well, between schoolwork and helping Mom around the house, I barely had time to go to school dances. Then, when I went to college, I realized we needed money, not a lot of it, but it ran our lives. So I had to work two jobs and pay for everything."

Anya gave him a shy smile. "Not many men consider being responsible sexy, you know. They want party girls and internet sensations."

"They're fucking idiots," Drake declared passionately.

Amazed no one had ever seen the light in her. The passion and the very decency that had attracted him to her in the first place. Even though she had been a thief in the night when they'd first met.

"Besides." She tucked her head against his shoulder. "I wasn't too keen on anyone too, Drake. They weren't…"

"What? Smart?" He teased her, kissing the side of her head. Smelling the lilies of her leave-in conditioner.

Anya nodded thoughtfully. "Smart, yeah. But they weren't…" She hesitated. "Have you ever felt like no one in the whole world could ever understand you, the things you want and are, even if you told them again and again?"

He nodded slowly. "Yes. Constantly."

"That's how I felt when I went out on dates. I wanted to talk about inflation price indices and they wanted to feel me up."

He grabbed her waist under the top and she rubbed like a little cat against him. "What makes you think I don't want to feel you up?"

Anya leaned up and nipped at his jaw. He felt the kiss sizzle under his skin all across his nerve endings. "You explain historical inflation price indices better than any professor I'd ever had. I want to feel *you* up, babe."

She grabbed his butt discreetly inching his jacket up and squeezed. He mock-growled as he tried to swat her hands away.

Anya was laughing, tossing hair out of her eyes. She looked happy.

She looked like what happiness could be for him. With her golden eyes, her lithe body and the wild curls of her hair. From the tips of her delicate fingers to the ends of her feet, she represented what he'd come to crave.

And he didn't know how to deal with it. Or even if what he was feeling was at all real. *Possible.*

Anya's laughter faded. "Drake? What's wrong?"

He shook his head. "Nothing's wrong. Everything's right." He gave her another smile, this one was heartfelt.

Because he'd just said the truth. Everything was alright. He was just waiting for the other shoe to drop because it was what he did in business. Looked at the shiniest possible option, immediately discarded it because it would lead to massive losses for everyone, and choose other options.

But Anya wasn't just a shiny option. She was the only possible option. Period.

"Here." He handed her his smart watch. Strapping it around her slender waist, over a sparkly plastic bracelet. "Use this to order dinner? I've programmed it so it responds to your commands. You can use this one till yours comes in from the R&D team."

Anya shook her head. "I've finally seen the impossible." She grinned cheekily. "Billionaire Drake Fallahil parts with his fancy watch."

"I'll show you fancy watch…" He grabbed her and tickled her elbow. She shrieked and fell against him. He continued mercilessly exploiting her weakness till she was breathless and laughing.

"Stop, *stop* it, Drake."

He swung her around, making her dizzy with his display of strength. "I'm not stopping till you cry please."

"Hello son."

Drake whirled around, Anya in his arms. And saw a specter, a ghost from a past he'd successfully left behind. Saw a nightmare come to life.

His knees went boneless, his fingers went numb. And he would have dropped Anya to the ground if she hadn't clung to him, sliding down his length.

Drake couldn't take his eyes off the old, haggard-looking man in the cheap grey suit. His heart roared like thunderous rainstorms in his ears. He could feel the familiar hiss and lash of the leather belt coming to hurt his skin.

His fingers contracted, painfully, against Anya's back.

"How did you find me, dad?" he asked quietly.

~ ~ ~ ~ ~

"Hello, Drake." Caleb Fallahil stepped out of the shadows of a great supertree and approached Drake slowly. Carefully. His steps slow and shuffled, as if he couldn't walk upright.

His iron grey hair was wispy in places, Drake noted dispassionately.

His eyes were watery, rheumy with age. And they were most definitely not the intense, savage blue that stared out of his own face every time he looked in the fucking mirror.

"I asked, how the fuck did you find me?"

Drake felt Anya touch his elbow. A butterfly-light touch. He wanted to shake her off. As rage, enormous, indescribable, and uncontained, filled every inch of him. He gave her one dark look.

"Leave," he ordered. "Now."

Anya's lips trembled. He knew she saw the thing in him dying to be unleashed. But she held onto his arm. "I'm not going anywhere. I'll be here. Okay?"

"Anya."

Anya touched his arm again, digging her fingers into his forearm. "I'll just order dinner for us. You talk and then we can leave, okay?"

He'd rolled up the jacket and shirt to his elbows, so they could hold hands and walk around a garden like a normal freaking couple. Forgetting what they were.

What he was.

What he'd always be.

The things she said made no sense to him. She expected him to have dinner? To walk away as if everything was okay. To not kill this man where he stood for daring to…

"Okay, Drake?" Anya commanded him.

She might have been a tiny thing but she had the strength of an Amazon in her. Because she didn't run. She stood there and she faced him down. Made him see past the fury of this moment.

"Listen to her son," Caleb said. "Your wife knows what she's talking about."

"You don't talk to her," Drake exploded. "You don't breathe near her. You don't think about her. You understand me, old man?"

Caleb took a step back.

Anya restrained Drake's quivering form with the gentle strength of her arms around his arm.

This time, Drake shook her off. Advancing toward the person, the being responsible for every bad thing that had ever happened to him. Anya forgotten in the wake of his fury.

~ ~ ~ ~ ~

"How did you find me, Caleb?" He spat. "Why did you? Was the money I sent you not enough? You only had to ask for more. I would have given that too. I didn't want to see you. Ever. You knew that."

"Yes." Caleb's rheumy eyes filled with tears. Making him look weak and small. Fallen. "You made that clear, Drake. But I had to see you."

"Why?" Drake was vaguely aware of Anya moving a few steps away, giving him the illusion of space. Of privacy.

He felt seared open, his every weakness, all his secret fears exposed for the world to see. Made flesh in the shape of the man who'd done this to him.

"Why?" He asked again, barely keeping his voice down. "You abandoned mom and me before I was born, didn't you? Didn't you feel like you had to see me then? Or any of the seventeen years before you found Lily and me again?"

Caleb's lips quivered under the bushy moustache he'd grown to cover his weak nose and weaker chin.

Drake felt nothing but towering contempt toward Caleb, saw how the progression of years had wrecked this man who was his father.

"I made a lot of mistakes, son. I know that. I've known that for years now. I just want to make amends now if you'd let me."

"Amends?" Drake was blessedly soft. "You want to make amends for the years that motherfucking bastard hit me for *existing*? Punishing me for being born? How can you?" His fists clenched.

"How can you make amends for the way that man treated mom?"

Caleb shook his head. "I know I can't. I know there's no excuse for it all…"

"Damn straight there isn't. It was a miracle she held out for as long as she did. And if it wasn't for Lily, I wouldn't have either, you *motherfucker.*"

Drake grabbed the old man by the collar of his polyester suit. Almost pulled him to his toes.

Unholy fury coursed through him, striking out of him everywhere it could escape. His fingers. His flaring nostrils. His toes clad in three-thousand-dollar wingtips. His very ears.

Caleb feebly batted at his hands. "Drake, please…"

Drake's chest heaved as he felt the old man's heart beat frantically against his rib cage. His eyes shifty and pale and full of shame.

"I will never forgive you for what you did to mom. To me," he vowed. "I've been paying you for the last two decades to stay the fuck away from me. I'll continue doing so but that is *all* you get, old man."

He dropped Caleb to his feet. The man stumbled before righting himself.

Drake had no inclination to help him. "I do not want to look at your cowardly, miserable face as long as I live."

Caleb looked stricken.

"And if you ever come near me or mine again, you'll know exactly what it is that you so casually birthed and abandoned, old man. Remember that," he finished in a quietly lethal voice.

His hands were in the pockets of his pants, because he didn't quite trust himself to not hit the old man. Pummel him into the very earth so he'd never rise up and haunt him again.

Caleb wiped inelegant, snotty tears from his streaming eyes. "I'm so sorry, Drake. I'm so sorry for everything."

"You should be." Drake turned away from him, finished with him in the only way he knew how to be.

"That's all I ever wanted to say to you," Caleb continued, sniffling. "That I'm sorry. It's what I wanted to say to you at Dev Banerjie's wedding. It was in the note I gave your wife. When you didn't reach out to me after reading it, I was…worried."

Drake looked at him incredulously, unable to believe his ears. "What the fuck are you talking about, Caleb?"

Caleb nodded at Anya, playing with the watch he'd given her just a few minutes ago. "I saw Anya in Chicago. Gave her a note to give you."

"You saw Anya…" Drake shook his head. "I don't believe you. You're lying."

"I am not…"

"And what's more," he said slowly. "Even if you weren't. I. Don't. Care about you." He spaced each word carefully, feeling the truth of them in his bones. In his very marrow. "You need to leave now. Before I call security and have you arrested for trespassing."

"This is public property. You don't own everything, Drake." Caleb waved a shaking hand about.

"Don't I?" Drake challenged him. Allowing him to feel the full weight of the man he'd become. Despite this man's influence. His blood coursing through him. "Can't I?"

Caleb looked like he was going to say something else. Then he thought better of it, and giving him a last regretful look, left.

~ ~ ~ ~ ~ ~

Drake turned away from Caleb and almost ran to Anya, who stood very still. Her eyes enormous in a face gone pale.

He ran restless shaking palms up and down her back, her sides. "You're okay? You're fine?"

"I'm fine," she said distantly. "I was just…" She made a flopping motion with one hand.

"I know." He tried to hug her, while holding the shakes in. "I'm so sorry you had to witness that."

"That's not your…that's not Lily's dad?" She asked vaguely.

He nodded. "Yeah, Caleb was a ranch hand from Texas who wandered into St. Cloud Minnesota for the sole purpose of carousing through town and wrecking my mother's life. She was a waitress at the local bar. They hooked up until she had me."

"I…"

"He hightailed out of town the second he found out Mom was pregnant. And it's a small town. God-fearing. People talk. Mom had to find some way out for herself."

"So she married Lily's father?" Anya supplied softly.

He nodded. "Yeah. Jack Fallahil was a regular at the bar too. He'd always had a soft spot for mom. It made sense for her to accept his proposal when he asked. Only, after they were married did he come to know she wasn't as virgin white as he thought she'd been and…well… he couldn't take it out on her because she was wide as a house."

"I'm so sorry." She ran a shaking hand down his chest. "I'm so sorry, Drake. This is awful to happen to anyone."

Drake gave a short harsh laugh. "You asked me why I quit high school to work at an oil rig the other day, right?

It's because the son of a bitch came back when Lily's father, the other son of a bitch, died. And Caleb wanted to 'take care' of Lily and me." He could feel the blood pulsing in him when he air-quoted take care. "I told him I'd pay for him to leave us the fuck alone."

Anya's lips trembled but she didn't cry. This woman was made of steel.

"You shouldn't have had to do that. You were just a young boy."

"I was never a young boy, Anya." He swallowed thickly. "I was never that innocent. All I ever wanted was to be so powerful so no Caleb or Jack would ever touch me or mine again."

She stepped closer to him and brushed her mouth against his cold lips. Her face was soft, giving, a gentle blessing in the shit-storm riding him. "I'm so proud of the man you are, Drake. I..." She paused deliberately. "Care so much about you."

Lightning struck drake, turning his veins into liquid fire because he knew she didn't mean this four-letter word but the other one. Panic, fear...hope, swelled in him in gargantuan proportions. To avoid having to answer the question in her eyes, he turned away. Grasped at the only thing making sense to him.

"My father..." Drake swallowed as he tried to parse the complex emotions he'd felt in the last five minutes.

All his life, if he was being honest with himself. And he couldn't. They were indescribable.

So, he latched onto the one glaring flaw in the old man's rambling. "That bastard told me something so ludicrous. He said he met you during Dev and Zara's wedding. Gave you some note." He laughed, a wild sound in the forest of green. "As if you'd ever talk to him, right?"

Anya didn't say a word. She just stared at him mournfully.

Disquiet leached the wild elation filling him. "Right, Anya?"

Her wrist beeped. Loudly. "That must be the restaurant," she murmured. Trying to look at the display.

Drake simply held tight to her wrist, not allowing her to check it. He opened his mouth to say something innocuous, but what emerged instead was, "My father wasn't lying about meeting you, was he?"

FOURTEEN

Anya reeled. Actually, there was no word in the English lexicon to describe the feelings careening inside her.

Shock and sympathy for Drake and his revelations. Fear at the unrestrained anger she'd seen pour out of him when he'd grabbed his father and raised him to his toes. She'd never seen a man with so much strength be so dangerous with it.

She couldn't understand how she loved a man so dangerous.

Because, under the fear and shock and sympathy and fury on his behalf for what Caleb had put Drake through for the simple fact of being born was love. A colossal love that was endless, scary in and of itself.

And she, who had thought herself to be the most responsible of people, was suddenly unmoored.

Undone by love for one man.

"Answer me, Anya," Drake said softly, his fingers biting into her arms. He still had a little bit of the manic in his wild eyes. "Tell me my father was lying."

"Why does it matter?" She asked him. "Didn't you tell him you didn't care what he said to me?"

"I don't care what he said to you," he said immediately. "I care that you kept it from me."

"I…" Anya bit her lip, staring up at him.

Seeing anew the lines near his eyes, the hard planes of his incredibly handsome face. The wrath he'd shown his dad still simmering in the edges of his eyes, flickering there like a living thing.

"What was I supposed to do, Drake? Do you remember what we were to each other in Chicago? You'd summoned me, *summoned* me," she repeated. "To attend the wedding of a family member. A member I didn't know existed. I was furious with you for it all."

"Fine," Drake bit off. "Fine. You were angry then. In Chicago. But what about after? What about every day since then, Anya? You had a whole month, all of this time, to tell me my father contacted you and you didn't."

His hands dropped from her hands, leaving her suddenly cold in the warm summer night.

He looked horrified. "Were you trying to manipulate me, Anya? Soften me towards the old man so I wouldn't kill him?"

"What?" She burst out. "I forgot about him the second he left my sight. I don't even remember the note he gave me."

She tried to recall that moment when Caleb had appeared in front of her and told her he was Bret's grandfather. Which was not *exactly* true because Lily was not his daughter. But, the truth was, she'd clean forgotten about him because she was too consumed by Drake.

Fighting with him. Understanding him.

Loving him.

"You're lying."

"No." She urgently shook her head. Tried to touch his arm. It was stone-hard under her touch.

"Drake, no," she said in a more reasonable tone.

Aware that one of them had to keep their calm and it seemed like that responsibility fell on her.

"I wasn't trying to manipulate you into being nice to your father. If I'd known he'd done all of this to you when we first met, I'd have bonked him over the head with the champagne bottle I'd finished."

Anya gave him a tentative smile. "He's not very sprightly. I could have done it too. Right?"

"If you weren't manipulating me, why would you…" He shook his head. So cool, so distant. "I don't understand why you kept this from me."

Anya kissed the tips of his fingers. "Maybe because I was trying to protect you. Someone has to, right?"

He was so quiet, so still. A black hole of nothingness. Colossus made flesh.

Tears shimmered in her eyes, gathering in the clutches of her throat. Because understanding dawned, quick and cruel.

"You don't believe me," she whispered.

"I don't understand you." Drake shook his head again, as if to clear it.

His crystal-bright eyes were unfocused. It was frightening to see. Because Drake was never less than one hundred percent certain.

The watch beeped again. This time, he didn't stop her as she lifted her wrist to check the display.

"This fucking restaurant…" Anya trailed off.

Her head swam as she saw the email sliding into the display. The subject line a clear bold statement of betrayal.

The first piece of her heart broke into an icy shard which stabbed her where she stood.

Her hair hid her face before she lifted it to face him. She looked as shocked as he felt. "Why do you have a letter of intent for purchasing the SG office complex signed by Runwal Realty, Drake?"

~ ~ ~ ~ ~

Drake looked at the elfin face of the woman he'd trusted the most, who'd so casually betrayed him. At least, it *felt* like she had betrayed him by keeping the fact of meeting Caleb from him.

After all, what motive could she have to protect him? He remembered. Vividly. How she'd come to his hotel room that very night, the night of Dev and Zara's wedding, seemingly a changed woman. Who'd wanted, no *demanded* things, answers… emotions from him. Even as she was doing so now.

What was that if not clear manipulation?

"Answer me, Drake," she said determinedly. "Tell me this isn't true."

"I don't lie, Anya," he replied. "I'm not about to."

She sucked in a short breath. Hurt filling her expressive eyes. "Why would you willingly do business with the people who tried to destroy my sister? Who sent her to jail, Drake?"

He folded his hands, looked down his nose at her. As the hot thrum of anger fled his heart, his brain, until clear, cool logic remained. His brain came back online. *Finally.*

"Why, Drake?"

"Why do you think, Anya?" he suggested. "It's good business. I wasn't going to let a little bit of personal destruction come between a profitable deal. I'm not a bleeding fucking heart, am I?"

Anya shook her head. "No," she said with quiet dignity. "A bleeding heart you're not."

"And before you think I'm the worst thing since the devil, maybe you should find out what your sister was really in jail for?" He spoke silkily. "You'll be surprised to hear what she has to say."

Anya's lips trembled. "You're just saying that to mess with my head. You're hurt by what happened with your father and you're taking it out on me. But, for all her faults, my sister and I are tight."

"Are you? Really?"

She began nodding but stopped because he said, "Then why did she not tell you about the sensors, Anya? If your sister was so tight with you. Why did she allow you to walk into a trap that would have allowed you to land your pert ass in jail?"

"She didn't know," Anya defended her swiftly. "Ishqi would never knowingly hurt me. Unlike you," she finished bitterly.

He touched her then. His fingers blessedly numb or he'd have wanted to sink his fingers into her waist. And hold on for dear life.

As it was, for the first time in two months, he felt like the Drake of old. In full control of himself. In full control of the situation.

In full control of his opponent.

"How am *I* hurting you, Anya?" He speared his hand into her wonderful hair. Gripped her skull.

"Because you don't believe me," she confessed on a jagged breath.

When he tried to bring her up for his kiss, she resisted. Tugging at his wrist ineffectually. No match for his superior strength.

"Don't you want me anymore?" he brushed the words against her lips.

"Not like this," Anya whispered. Begged. "Drake, please. Not like this."

He thrust her away from him. "Why not? What else do you want from me?"

"I want you to tell me the truth," she shot back aggressively, her voice, even her slender shoulders shaking from the force of her passion. "Why are you going into business with Ajay Runwal when you know he's a shady, evil bastard?"

And, Drake knew why he was saying the things he was saying. What decision his brain, no, his *heart* had reached before he'd even become aware of it.

He was going to untether Anya from him. By making her hate him like he deserved to be.

"Because," Drake replied calmly. "So am I, Anya. I'm a shady, evil bastard. Haven't you figured that out yet?"

Her lips parted, her chest heaved, and he was filled with raging desire, even worse, tenderness and most of all...the certainty of the knowledge that this was right. This was meant to be. The way she looked at him.

With scorn and fear...uncertainly, this was exactly the way it was supposed to be.

"I don't believe you. You're just saying that to push me away. You're starting The Verdant Fund. You're *good*, Drake."

Drake shook his head. Brought her closer to him by simply hooking one hand in the waistband of her shorts. "I'm not. The Verdant Fund's just good business. I have to survive the apocalypse that's coming and going green, supporting green is the only way to do so. I'm not good, Anya. But I think you have me mistaken for someone else."

"Who?" Her eyes were so enormous, as they swallowed the rest of her face.

"A hero," Drake said softly. "You think I'm the hero of this story. I'm not."

Anya swallowed, a convulsive movement of her throat.

"I'm not a hero, Anya," he repeated. "The only reason I'm trying to fix this world with a four trillion hedge fund that is probably not going to fix it anyway is because I'm the reason it broke in the first place. Check the stable of companies I'm invested in. See our carbon-footprint, how they treat their employees and you'll know."

He leaned down and whispered silkily. "Money. Profit. It's what drives me, Anya."

Her breath broke out in a sob. "Don't say that," she said in a low voice. "Don't use your good and noble work and your father to punish yourself, Drake. Don't do that to me."

"I'm not," he said softly. "I really am not. But the thing is…if that's how you see me, then you don't understand me at all, do you? Even though I told you over and over again, who I was? I told you the truth."

Anya's trembling lips firmed. And one hot tear fell down her cheek. She made no effort to wipe it away.

"Yes," she said tiredly. "You did. I just thought…I thought you knew it was okay to change."

"I am what I am, Anya. Change isn't for me." And he believed it, sincerely.

Because looking at his father, the horror to have had birthed him and left him to fend for himself in a cruel, hopeless world had made that fact abundantly clear to him.

He had to be alone. Forever. So he didn't pass on the cowardice and the weakness and the horror to someone else. Tainted them with it.

Anya smiled, a small heartbreaking smile. "Then there's nothing else to say, is there?"

"No," he agreed. "I suppose there isn't."

"Okay, then." Anya stared at him for a long, endless moment.

Then she reached up and pressed a kiss on lips gone numb. "Goodbye, Drake Fallahil. I hope you forgive yourself one day and see yourself like I see you."

For the first time, he didn't kiss her back. He couldn't.

She squeezed his hand, dropping down to her toes. She gave him a soft, warm, yearning look. "Because you're the best man I know. You're the man I lo…"

Anya sniffed. Tears fell down her face. Then she whirled on sneakered feet and ran out of the Garden as if the devil himself was after her.

But the devil stood there on legs gone numb and watched the best thing in his life run away from him.

Because the devil, Drake acknowledged, was ruinous. And beyond absolution.

FIFTEEN

"Die, demon bitch. Die by my hands!" Anya yelled as she held the gun steady in both hands and pressed the trigger in a rat-tat-tat motion.

The demon bitch exploded in a satisfying burst of red with bits of bone and gristle scattering everywhere.

Anya pumped one fist high. The rush of adrenalin mixed with the manic smile on her face, making her feel like the Celts might have when they faced down the Viking horde.

She lowered the gun so it swung idly in her hands. Waited for the six-feet-tall screen in front of her to stop showering confetti and return back to the next level of the game she was playing. It was, apropos called, Marauding Monster Mash, and she was killing it.

A slow clap penetrated through the pulse pounding rock pouring through the speakers. Her jam was Matchbox 20, old school nineties hits.

She turned around, blinking to adjust to normal lighting after staring at a 108K million screen in full rendered resolution. Tito's Video Arcade off Sentosa

Island did provide the best and most realistic gaming entertainment in the city.

"Vijay, I need an hour more, man," she called out. "I'm going to give this Marauding Monster the beat down it deserves."

~ ~ ~ ~ ~

"So bloodthirsty, sis," Ishqi commented, whistling.

She wore surprisingly adult clothes, although her jeans were more ripped than had fabric and her crop top had Cock written across the books, with the O and C cut out with fabric.

"Splurging for the private room I see. I guess you want to avoid being papped since you're slumming in this part of town." She strolled into the private room Anya had booked for the day.

The pricing was a little steep for the private gaming set up but worth it.

The chair alone was a special order XZ3 hackers used in Russia, designed for optimum lumbar and cranial support without sacrificing metacarpal action. Loosely translated, it helped with maintaining posture while allowing one to kill an astonishing number of video game monsters.

Besides, Anya did want to be alone. Away from people, in general.

People sucked.

The gun turned a little sweaty in Anya's hands as she clocked her sister. "How did you find me?"

She ignored the jibe about being papped, since it so did not apply to her anymore. She was ordinary, nothings-special Anya Mallya-Bhatt forevermore.

Ishqi held up her phone. "Find My Friend?"

Anya took her phone out. The screen was littered with notifications. Texts, voice messages, missed calls from Mili Iyer and the office.

She threw it in the trash. "Don't find me again."

The screen populated with the next level of the game. Anya turned around and took aim, waiting for the next round of bad guys to fill her vision.

So. She. Could. Kill. Them. All.

"Mom's worried about you, Anya," Ishqi said quietly. "She sent me here to find you."

Anya gave her a grim look. "Role reversal's a bitch, isn't it?"

Ishqi gave her a sardonic smile. "I agree. But I wanted to come find you anyway, Anya."

Anya shot off a four-headed scorpios demon on the screen. Taking aim between each pair of eyes so four heads exploded into mush at the same time. Her online avatar knelt down and did a chef's kiss pose.

"Nice! Really classy." Ishqi gave her a sideways glance. "*Sant* Anya." Saint in Hindi.

Anya kept the growl that wanted to tear out of her throat inside. "I'm no saint, Ishqi."

"Nope," Ishqi agreed. "I can hardly call you a saint when you just took on a bounty to rid the Land of Monsteria off monsters. That's not very saintly of you." Her unpainted lips twitched in obvious amusement.

"Where did you get the idea I'm a saint anyway?" Anya muttered.

Her sister's laugh, her smile, the very normalcy of her presence grated on her nerves. Reminded her that a world existed outside of this bloodthirsty, VR-created haven.

"Because." Ishqi clicked on a button on her phone and the screen froze. It fucking froze. "You always do the right thing. No matter how painful it is. You do it. It's in your blood."

Anya glared at her in frustration. "What did you do to the screen?"

Ishqi shrugged. Tucked her phone into the tight pocket of her jeans. "I just messed with the WiFi in this place. Don't worry, I'll fix it as soon as am done talking to you."

"Fine." Anya threw the gun on the chair with enough force that it bounced a couple times before settling on the deep cushion that had been such a support for her butt. "Talk!"

She grabbed a can of yellow Gatorade and gulped it down thirstily. The sugar water stuck to the sides of her throat, not melting the hard rock of grief and regret and rage created there ten days ago.

Ten days since she'd run, no *left* a certain conscience-less devil in a garden that smelled of hope and happy ever after, after he'd broken her heart so thoroughly there was no hope of repairing it.

~ ~ ~ ~ ~

"That." Ishqi snatched the bottle from Anya's hold. "That look in your eye is why I'm here."

Anya shot her a murderous look. "Give me back my Gatorade."

Ishqi held it up high, as high as she could go, and since she wore spike heeled boots she was at least four inches taller than Anya in her practical running shoes.

Anya cursed and stopped jumping up for the drink. She knew when to give up now on hopeless causes.

"Anya." Ishqi sighed and handed the drink back to Anya. "Mom found a scholarship application for the London School of Economics' business program under your bed. She thinks you're crying all the time. In your room. In here. And you won't tell her what happened with you and…your husband so she's worried. Don't you care about her? Why are you doing this to her?"

Anya burst out laughing. It was spontaneous, slightly hysterical but she couldn't help it. "First off, let's get something straight here. I don't have a husband. I never did."

It really helped to say that out loud. To not have the skies fall down on her head because a cold ember of hope still remained that it was all a dream. But the skies remained firmly situated.

"Secondly, I am not crying. I will never cry over that selfish, cowardly, *evil* bastard." She ticked off the pejoratives in her hand. "And lastly, Ishqi. You don't care about me. You never did. Mom doesn't need me now that she's ambulatory. What I do with my life is my business, isn't it?"

Ishqi stared at her thoughtfully. "So, you're using our bad behavior to justify your own?"

Anya's lips trembled as the barb struck home. Pierced the wall of denial, rage and righteousness she'd erected around her heart. "Fuck off, Ishqi, I don't want to talk to you anymore. There's nothing left to say between us."

"Really?" Ishqi sounded incredulous. "That's how you're going to be from now on?"

The last tether of control snapped inside Anya. All the rage spilled out at Ishqi's hurt tone. What did Ishqi have to be hurt about? Ishqi's world did not end. She wasn't *alone.* She wasn't…

Anya whirled around. "No. I have a few things to say to you. Get your shit together, sister. You can't be a hacker forever. One of these days you're going to end up in real trouble, the kinds even your poor gullible sister can't bail you out of. And you'll find yourself dead or worse."

"I wasn't…" Ishqi automatically protested.

"I don't care," Anya cut her off ruthlessly. "I don't care what reasons you have for doing the things you do. Your brain is ten times smarter than mine and mine's magnificent." Her voice wobbled at the word as a flash of endless, lightning blue filled her head.

She straighter her spine and continued. "Put it to some good fucking use. Legal use. I am not your keeper anymore. I'm tired of being the damned saint. You get me?"

Ishqi nodded. "I do, Anya. I get it. I came here to apologize, actually. I know now that…I am to blame for what happened to you. That I'm selfish and thoughtless. And you deserve better. A better sister."

Anya's lips parted as some of the air was punctured out of her sails. "Did you just apologize to me, Queen Ishqi?"

Ishqi turned in a restless movement. "Mom's had a talk with me. A few talks actually. She thinks, we both took advantage of your goodness and turned you into an old woman before your time."

Anya shook her head, her lips twitching in the semblance of a smile. While some of the venom leaching the life out of her drained away. Because Ishqi sounded earnest, sincere.

Vulnerable.

"Okay, I've fallen asleep here and I'm dreaming this shit up. You can't be serious."

Ishqi reached out and hugged Anya, slowly. Bending down at the waist and squeezing her arms around her. "Would this happen in your dream?"

Anya stood rigid for a minute before unbending. She wrapped her arms around her sister. Her shoulder and forearm sang with pain after being in the same position for hours as she took out the last demon bitch.

"Ouch, this hurts. Okay, no dream," she murmured.

Ishqi grinned at her. Soft and hopeful. "Does this mean you forgive me?"

Anya cocked her head. "Only if you help me beat this monster scum using your skills."

They broke the hug and Ishqi's smile faded. "About that…I wanted to tell you…I'm going to retire from the business."

"You are?"

She ran a hand through her corkscrew curls. Tangling into them with pointed fingers. "That's actually what the deal with the Runwals was about. I wasn't entirely honest with you, Anya."

She gave Anya a contrite look.

And, unwittingly, Anya remembered what *he'd* said the last time they'd spoken.

Maybe you should find out what your sister was really in jail for…

"Tell me," Anya commanded. "Everything."

Ishqi sighed. "I knew the Runwals were shady as fuck. That they'd come by several of their latest development deals illegally. I just didn't know how. I thought it was because they were laundering money for some mob outfit. But their racket is so ridiculously simple. They just use someone like me each time they bid on a large project, look at their competitor's financials and severely undercut it."

"Undercut it?"

Ishqi shrugged. "They bribe someone on the inside to give them the figures on tender bids. And then go on a significantly lower bid to win the contract. It's a genius system, actually."

Anya thought it through. "But they can't be making any profit then. They can't even afford to finish the projects under budget because obviously it's impossible to do this every single time."

Ishqi nodded. "Precisely. It is impossible. So they turned to insurance fraud to cover up their losses. A fire here, a roadspill accident there. A worker falling down to his death in tragic circumstances…"

"And they get extensions on their deadlines, plus insurance money and they can charge more than they would have initially to pay the insurance premiums for their clients," Anya concluded, her brain racing at the speed of light, connecting all the dots.

"Yes. This stuff is not recorded anywhere in their public servers, especially the money that's funneled offshore from the insurance payouts," Ishqi confirmed the next logical step of their scam. "When I tried to talk to Ajay about it, he trumped up some bullshit charge against me and had me thrown in jail."

"So you wanted me to break into their personal, guarded server and get you the evidence."

"I did." Ishqi gave her a miserable look. "I'm so sorry, Anya. It's unforgivable that I did that to you. You shouldn't have to pay for my mistakes."

"But I didn't," Anya reminded her icily. "I was rescued by…" Unbidden, she recalled the first time she'd seen Drake Fallahil. A black hole in a sea of gyrating stars.

Still. Complete. Alone.

She shook her head to clear the memory. "Anyway. I wasn't thrown in jail too. But the problem still remains. The Runwals are still walking around free instead of paying for their crimes."

With sinking horror, she realized how free the Runwals were.

They'd just been awarded one of the biggest development projects of their lives – the four trillion dollar, Verdant Fund. A beautiful, perfect, blameless creation. And so what if the man who'd conceived of it was no better than them, the project deserved to come to fruition, untainted by the corrupt greed of a few vile men.

She'd worked too damn hard on it, bar the last ten days, for it to be shunted away because of corruption charges.

"The Runwals can't work on any projects anymore," Anya muttered. "They…it's not fair."

Ishqi nodded. "Yeah. I kind of have a plan to rectify that."

Anya nodded, determination hardening her face and heart. Straightening her spine, changing the shape of her slumped body. "Tell me what we're going to do."

So, Ishqi told her.

SIXTEEN

A few hours later, Anya and Ishqi were camped out in a tiny Citroen whose dashboard was tricked out to hold monitoring and recording equipment. Right at the corner Tanjong Pagar's supermarket.

The transceiver stingray antenna was apparently from a producer in Taiwan, looking to branch into surveillance from microchips. The stingray was meant to capture all electronic chatter – texts, calls, camera media, computer files, and traffic cam video. Ishqi had fiddled with it so the range of the antenna went from one hundred feet to one hundred meters.

Anya wore the headphones that Ishqi handed her with trepidation. She was dressed in thief's black, with a cap to hide her distinctive hair.

"Remind me once again why we can't go to the authorities with our suspicions, Ishqi?"

Ishqi grunted as she finished taping the skin-colored wire to her bosom and tugged her sexy tank top in place over it. The receiver was tucked under the bottom of her micro-mini, a tiny thing, hardly one inch in diameter and easily hidden. "Because, right now all we have are suspicions. We need proof to take to the authorities."

She tapped the wire snaking through her, almost an exact match to her dusky, golden skin tone. "I get Ajay Runwal to confess on tape to how he paid me off, when I meet him in seven minutes. We have our proof and the fuckers can go to jail for a long, long time."

"Or hire expensive lawyers who'll get them off with a plea deal," Anya countered.

"Either way, their reputation and credibility will take a hit. And that's good enough isn't it?" Ishqi argued logically.

Anya thought about The Verdant Fund, the most ambitious, insanely good thing to come in global business for years to come. A project that would benefit seventeen different countries because one man had decided to do some good with the wealth and resources he had at his disposal.

Sometimes, the ends did justify the means.

"Yes," she agreed quietly. "It's good enough."

And it was.

Ishqi hopped out of the Citroen, adjusting her skirt which had ridden up indecently high. She was decked up in a purple tank glittering with a unicorn that matched her suede leather skirt. Her makeup was as Ishqi as ever – bold eyes, bolder lips, and huge spangled earrings to complete the quasi cam girl look.

"We'll get the bastards, Anya."

"Try and not get killed, Ishqi," Anya sighed. "Mom will never forgive me if I got you killed."

"Well," Ishqi blew her a soft, winking kiss. "You can tell mom I died for a good cause."

Anya gave her the finger, which turned into a waggle of fingers signifying, Love You, at the last moment.

Then she settled back to wait for the sting to be set in motion.

~~~~~

In theory, this was not a half-bad plan. Her sister had, for once, covered all their bases.

The equipment was top-notch. The location safe enough so no one could try anything. The car they were in was not registered to either of them. It was parked a long distance away from the Runwals' penthouse where Ishqi had asked Ajay to meet her.

She'd used a burner phone to contact Ajay Runwal, that criminal mofo. And, the man had agreed to meet her, reluctantly, which solidified his guilt as far as Anya was concerned.

In theory, this was a five-minute job at the most.

But a lot could go wrong in five minutes, couldn't it?

After all, she'd gone from being in love with a wonderful man to disastrously heartbroken in the space of five minutes.
~~~~~

Anya sighed, adjusted the phones against her head one more time. Checking to see if she was visible to passersby. It was only eleven pm so the street was still hopping but not as much as it would be if they'd done this in peak evening traffic.

Ishqi had actually outdone herself with planning this sting.

She was determined to not think about her own sorry love life, preferring to focus on literally anything that would keep the tears at bay. But what was worse than the tears was the knowledge that maybe Drake was right.

Maybe she'd tried to make him into something he was not. Because she couldn't fathom how she'd fallen for a dark, dangerous, ruthless man. One who claimed to have no heart.

What did that say about her, then? That she needed to convince herself it was love to enjoy head-banging sex with a terrible person. How pathetic was that?

~ ~ ~ ~ ~

"I'm in position," Ishqi's voice came through loud and clear.

Anya stopped brooding. "Great. Is Runwal there?"

"Yeah," Ishqi answered. "He's getting out of the parking structure elevators. He's reaching into his pocket. Shit, Anya! He's carrying a…"

Anya heard something metallic ping softly in her ear. She clutched at her headphones.

"Ishqi? Ishqi!" She screamed. "What the fuck happened, Ishqi?"

She tried to scramble out of the car, almost falling to the pavement.

A sharp pain exploded in her temple when someone strong and male grabbed her by the ends of her hair. Hauled her up so she dangled like landed trout on struggling legs. One of her shoes fell from her socked feet, and she didn't even know it.

Jay Runwal, the dumb twin, the good twin, held her captive in a bruising hold.

Impeccably dressed in a charcoal grey suit, with not a gelled hair out of place, he smiled pleasantly at her. "My brother shot your sister, Ms. Mallya-Bhatt. That's what the fuck happened."

Anya took a deep breath to scream her impressive lungs out. Even as fear and terror and a thousand emotions congealed thick in her stomach, immobilizing her for a single precious second.

He produced a hypodermic needle and plunged it into the vein beating so thickly at her neck.

"Sleep now, Anya," he said softly.

Anya's eyes rolled back in her head as the sedative coursed through her, hitting her bloodstream in an epic rush. Her thoughts were in immediate turmoil, spinning in circles, until they became a single name she wasn't allowed to think anymore.

"Resistance is futile," Jay ended.

Anya slumped against her captor, and he stashed her in the car she didn't own, started it and drove away in it. While the world spun by, with no one the wiser.

SEVENTEEN

"Hey, dummy." Mili threw a water bottle at Drake's sweaty back. "We need to talk. *NOW.*"

Drake paid her no attention at all as he continued shadow boxing in the ring of the gym at Oceania Park. It was nearly midnight, so the whole building was deserted. He could listen to the music of his choice while he kickboxed, punched, punching bag'd, and generally punished his body beyond human limits with no one bothering him.

So far, it was working exactly as it should.

He flashed one hand out, watched as the skin rippled with sweat and pain sang up and down his deltoids. It *hurt.* But not enough.

"Drake. Are you listening to me? Can you stop for a minute?"

No, he couldn't. He couldn't stop. Because stopping would mean thinking and thinking was forbidden. Not required. Done.

Yes, done was the word. Not forbidden.

Forbidden would mean he had no control over himself and needed to deny himself. But he wasn't denying himself anything. He was simply...done. He'd been done for the last ten days and ten nights.

Ten wretched days and ten unending, sleepless nights...

"Hey." This time she hit him with something harder than a water bottle.

It made him pause. He turned around. Every single muscle and bone in his body protesting at the movement. His neck felt so heavy, his knees were rubbery. But the ache, the fucking ache in his heart would not *go away.*

Drake clenched his fists in the boxing gloves, felt the tape tear through his bruises. Bleed inside. The pain was kind, a balm to the ache in his heart. The ache he'd brought upon himself because he'd finally confronted the truth of the man he actually was.

Mili slipped off her five-inch Jimmy Choos, stepped inside the ring, bending through the ropes. An anomaly in the quiet, punishing world he'd created for himself.

There had to be a word for this, wasn't it? Could it be hell?

"Go away," he growled at her.

"Not until we talk, boss." She handed him a piece of paper.

He didn't take it. Mostly because opening his fists required effort he did not possess at the moment. He just stared at her coolly. "What is this, Mili?"

"My letter of resignation. Effective immediately."

Her words were condemning, scornful. So was her face. Stunning in its own way now that he thought about it. Now that he noticed her as a person, and not as a perfect means to the ends he'd tried to build for himself.

"I see." He nodded. "I accept, of course."

She threw it at his chest, chest heaving. Her aim eerily accurate. "Fuck you, Drake. Why aren't you fighting me on this?"

He rubbed at the ache in his chest. It had intensified when she threw the letter at him. Another example of the prime way he'd fucked things up for people he cared about. "My therapist tells me I'm too controlling. I need to…" He opened his fist. "Loosen up."

His bones hurt. But so did all of him. He deserved it.

Mili rolled her eyes, although some of the hurt and anger left her. "While no one's happier than I am that you're finally getting the help you deserve, I have to stop you from killing yourself."

"I am not getting the help I deserve. I'm…" Purging myself. Reshaping the things inside me. Dark and poisonous and ugly things only designed to hurt the people I love.

Drake stared unseeing at her. He turned his back to her, because having her here was wrecking his fragile peace. Was making him want for other things. Things he couldn't, in all good conscience, have anymore.

People he had no right to anymore.

Mili touched his shoulder and he tensed. She'd inadvertently touched his scar.

Drake wanted to shake her off, because the scar was… just a scar. The scar was just a part of his life. His body. A map to the war he'd fought and won. The scar had been the subject of his first session with the therapist nine days ago. It had been intense. Uncomfortable.

Unmanned him.

He'd vowed to not go back.

He'd gone back every single day.

There was so much to atone for. Heal from.

"What do you want to talk about, Mili?" He was tired. He had to get things done. So many things had to be done before he could begin to think of the only thing he wanted to.

The only *person*.

~ ~ ~ ~ ~ ~

"Anya," Mili said hardily.

Drake gave her a misery-filled look. "Damn you, Mili. Damn you."

Mili shook her phone in his face. "She's not returned a single one of my calls, texts or voice messages. Not *one*, Drake. What did you do to her that she won't talk to me?"

I knowingly broke her heart because I want to save her from being with me.

He shook his head. Sweat dripped over his eyes. "Why haven't you visited her, then? If you're so concerned about her?" And tell me how she looks. Whether she still smiles with her whole body…

"I have some pride, you know," Mili muttered. She sat down on the sweaty foam pads on the ring. Her long legs flowing under her, because she did power yoga three times a week.

She gave him a sad look. "You screwed up on purpose, didn't you?"

Drake slowly untangled his box and looked absently at the bloody tapes on his hand. They seeped blood upon blood. Still he felt no better than he had when he'd started two hours ago.

When would it get better?

"Dr. Jeong says I have abandonment issues coupled with trust issues so I avoid deep and lasting attachments and control all outcomes."

"Like proposing marriage to a woman you were instantly crazy about instead of, I don't know, asking her out on a real date?" Mili suggested wryly.

He gave her another hang dog look. "I thought you were trying to help me."

"I am." Mili tugged at his hand. Took over the task of unwrapping the tapes. "You know, when I first took up my position with you, my predecessor left me a post-it note. It said, Welcome to Hell."

He chuckled mirthlessly. "Yes, this is hell."

"I thought it hilarious. Because you've always been so awesome to me, to everyone, Drake," Mili said softly.

He shook his head vehemently. "You *know* I haven't, Mili."

"Yes," Mili countered. "You have. You're a great boss. You're super understanding of the global concerns affecting locals of the whole *world.* And, in your own misguided alpha way, you tried to court Anya."

And there her name was. Again. Sneaking into his heart. Beating there like life's blood. His absolution and damnation twisted into a weight he couldn't shake off and didn't want to keep anymore. Because it fucking *hurt.*

"The stupid thing is, I think because of your childhood, you decided a long time ago that you're not worthy of love. Of any of the good things you offer the world. You live in massive denial so you don't have to face the truth."

"And what's the truth, Baby Yoda?"

Mili sighed and kissed his bloodied cheek. "That you're human. Fallible. But you're capable of redeeming yourself too. Because you've the best heart of anyone I've ever had the privilege to know."

"You don't mean…"

"I do," she said softly. Firmly. "I do, Drake. My predecessor was wrong about you. And so is the whole world. So's Aster and Robert Chan. I don't think you're denying yourself Anya. I think…you're scared she saw you for who you are. Like me, except you have sexy times with her."

He gave her a droll look.

"What?" She matched his look with a smug one of her own. "How in the world do you think I managed to stay on for the last seven years with you? It wasn't because of your fluffy personality or your epic money management skills. It's because you're the big brother I want," she said softly.

"You're not nice. But you're right. And you're kind. And you'd have fired me years ago if I'd said any of this to you," she finished accurately.

He rubbed at his chest again where a different kind of ache took root. One born of the need to hear her say these wonderful things about him. Even though, of course, they were untrue. Patently and ridiculously untrue.

"Mili…"

"Get Anya back," she said instead. "Do it. She's the only one apart from me and your sister who knows you. Who understands you, Drake. That's worth being scared for, isn't it?"

It was. He'd gladly cut open a vein and bleed in front of her if he thought it would help his cause. That would make things right between them. But…

"I'm too old for her." It wasn't an important reason but the differences between their years did bother him from time to time. She had so much of her life to live while he'd wasted so much of his trying to bend the world to his infernal will.

"Bull. Shit." Mili answered succinctly. "Anya's wise beyond her years and a functional adult. She knows what she wants." "Next?"

"I'm not worthy of her, Mili," he admitted gruffly. "I never was. I blackmailed her, threatened her, literally claimed my way into her life because that's what I do. I…" He swallowed. "I was so awful to her. So many times."

"Then make it up to her now, dummy," she suggested. "Anya loves you. I know she does. She was so miserable when you went on that totally trumped up trip all those weeks ago."

The night after he'd taken her in his office. The office he couldn't use anymore because she was there. Haunting him. She haunted him at the penthouse too. But then again, she was everywhere. Like an idea, a virus out of his control.

"And when you commanded her to come to Chicago, you know what the first expression on her face was?"

"Homicide?" He smiled wryly.

Mili shook her head. "Hope."

Hope. Drake was struck dumb by the idea that the woman he'd treated so badly, done so many terrible things to would still be hopeful when it came to him. That she would still want to be with him.

But she'd done it, hadn't she?

She'd chosen to be with him. Over and over and over again.

She'd chosen to stay with him after he'd told her about his childhood. She'd loved him then.

Why couldn't he accept that love and return it with all the fierceness of his beating heart? Because that was the ache in his chest. The definition of it. The cause and effect of it.

His heart beat. For the first time in his long, lonely, and misbegotten life his heart beat. Because he was in love with the finest, purest woman he'd had the privilege to meet. And he wouldn't change it for all the aches in the world.

And maybe, just maybe he didn't have to.

"There you go." Mili patted his sweaty hand. "That was the same goofy expression on her face too."

Hope, Drake realized.

It did not kill you. Even if you wanted to let it. No, it made you feel alive. Stronger. Better.

Like she did him.

And that was worth fighting for, right?

Renewed purpose filled him with a sudden burst of adrenalin.

No, he decided. This wasn't scientific. Biological. It was…celestial.

Like the doctor would say, this was fate giving him a chance to break old patterns and forge a new path for himself. Where he could simply choose to be worthy, by working for it every day. As long as it took to convince her she was it for him.

But for that -

"I have to go see Anya," he decided.

"My favorite dummy." Mili nudged his shoulder affectionately. "I knew I could get through to you better than any therapist."

Drake grinned. It probably bordered on feverish but he didn't care. He had a happy ever after to arrange.

"Thank you, my sister from another mister."

He leaned down and kissed her cheek. "Someday, some man is going to look into your wide heart and fall so deeply he won't find his way out again. He'll be the second-luckiest man to love you, Mili Iyer."

Mili blinked, pleased and befuddled. "Wow. That was…"

"Poetic, I know. I'm inspired."

He jumped down from the ring and went to retrieve his phone on the bench, beside his sweaty and smelly gym bag. It also contained his rumpled suit, the one he'd worn for two days straight. Because he couldn't bear to go home and face his empty apartment.

"I like this new side of you," Mili declared. She jumped down lightly too.

"I'm hoping so will…" Drake absently thumbed his phone open.

His blood froze. The world froze as he stared at the message on his phone.

~ ~ ~ ~ ~

Runwal has snatched Anya. Trying to triangulate his location now. She slipped my watch. Crafty sister. – Shane. Attached was a picture of a running shoe he'd recognize anywhere.

Anya's size six, dirty white off-brand sneaker.

"What's wrong, Drake? Drake, what's wrong? You're going to crack the phone." Mili tried to unpeel his hand from the phone. She read the message on his screen silently, grimly.

Thoughts, possibilities, solutions ran through his mind. While his brain tried frantically to think of a way to make this right.

And his heart was caught up in one sentence. *Runwal has snatched Anya.*

Mili quickly, efficiently messaged Shane back. "You're taking a shower. I'm contacting the authorities. Then we're meeting Shane and getting Anya back. Of course, we are."

His eyes burned with unshed tears, fearful tears. Because he knew why Runwal had Anya. He'd known and he'd done nothing to prevent this tragedy from occurring.

"I…"

"You can flagellate yourself. *After* we get Anya back. You still have to grovel at her feet," Mili said coolly. "Or were you lying to me, sir?"

And that was it. The clincher.

Drake Fallahil never lied. Not ever.

He shook his head. "No. I wasn't. Let's get the woman I love back from those murderous, thieving asshole pair of fucks."

EIGHTEEN

Anya came to in a pain-filled breath. There was a ringing in her ears, while someone had stuffed cotton in her mouth. She tried to blink her eyes open but couldn't. Something blinded her.

Terror pounded hot and heavy, immediate, in her heart. Right under the rib cage.

Ishqi! The thought exploded in the primal part of her brain.

Oh, god. Where was Ishqi!

She tried to turn her head this way and that, became aware of the zip ties binding her hands behind her back. When she stretched her neck, her shoulders zinged with pain.

Someone ripped off the blindfold from her eyes.

Anya sucked in a harsh gasp of air. The world swung crazily for a moment. Then it righted itself, colors and shapes blurring into coherence. And she saw her captor.

Jay Runwal. In an empty room of some sort. A single light bulb swung crazily between them in a parody of an interrogation room adding to the nightmare scenario.

Anya could barely make out shapes moving to the side, but she could not mistake the snick of guns being cocked. The safeties snapped off.

He grinned at her. In apparent relief. "Oh, thank god, you're awake Ms. Mallya-Bhatt. I thought I'd calibrated the dose incorrectly."

She gave him the most venomous of glares. "Where's my sister, you bastard? Where is she?" Anya screamed. "Ishqi! ISHQI!"

Jay simply reached out and grabbed her chin roughly. He shut her mouth by pressing her lips closed. The genial smile still played on his lips.

He let go of her mouth. "Your sister is not dead, of course. We aren't murderers, you know."

Anya spat at his face.

All the geniality fled from Jay's face and he clapped once.

One of the guards with guns stepped forward and butted the end of their submachine gun on Anya's cheek.

"Each time you disrespect me, I'll ask one of my people to hurt you," he spoke conversationally. "If you do it more than twice, I'll make them hurt Ishqi."

Anya felt faint. Anger and terror had her going dizzy, or maybe it was the after effect of the sedative he'd pumped her with. But Anya was nothing if not smart. She knew when to fold her cards and quit the game.

"I'll cooperate once I know Ishqi's okay."

He inclined his smarmy, gelled head. "Very well."

Jay clapped twice.

Anya had the insane urge to laugh. He was truly taking this villain act to heart. But she kept her mouth shut, her cheek stinging from the force of the blow.

Two more gun-toting guards dragged Ishqi between them. She lolled, unable to walk without support. A steady trickle of blood fell from her right arm. She was pale from blood loss and hardly able to talk.

"I'm so sorry," she whispered when she saw Anya.

She slumped on the floor, next to Anya, while the guards bound her wrists and legs with zip ties. She was crying steadily, her makeup streaking all over her lovely face.

Anya took a trembling breath because her first concern was alleviated. Ishqi was alive. Breathing. Everything else could be figured out.

"It's going to be fine," she promised her sister.

Even though she knew it wouldn't be. The problem with underestimating a sick fuck like Jay Runwal was that they could do anything. And Jay wanted to kill them both regardless of what he'd just said.

"Of course, it is," Jay said sweetly. "I am a reasonable man. I don't want to cause anyone undue harm."

"No," Anya said evenly. "You're the reasonable twin." She took a shot in the dark. "Your brother's the crazy one who shot my sister."

Jay's eyes flashed. "On my orders. My brother would never have the fucking brains to think of this plan all by himself."

Anya's hunch paid off. She pretended to sniffle, even as she tried to desperately figure out if Ishqi's wire had been ripped from her.

If she was a corrupt real estate developer, she'd search the shady hacker trying to shake her down.

"I don't understand," she said in a trembling voice that wasn't super hard to pull off.

She was genuinely scared. Terrified. For her sister. For herself.

"What don't you understand?"

She pushed sweaty and tangled hair from her cheek with a shrug. "What was your plan, Mr. Runwal?"

Jay knelt down and ran a hand down her cheek. Pressed into the bruise blooming there.

Anya knew he wanted her to feel hurt so she allowed the hurt to show in her eyes, on her face. She parted her lips on a pained breath.

"My plan was simple," Jay said simply. "We'd use your sister to do what we always did. Figure out the exact bids of our competitors. This time, ten percent of four trillion was at stake. That's an astronomical figure, Anya. Enough to kill, am I right?"

She swallowed. He was talking about The Verdant Fund project. The office complex Drake wanted to build here.

"But…my sister did more than that, didn't she?" She asked softly. "She figured out how your business really operated. With the insurance scam and everything."

Jay nodded. "Yeah. Your sister's the brightest hacker we've hired. I told Ajay not to hire her, she came too highly recommended. But he wouldn't listen. He wanted to bag Fallahil's project so badly."

Drake. Anya struggled to keep from reacting when the madman mentioned Drake's name.

Drake who'd never know how much she'd loved him when she died. Drake who didn't want her to love him so he'd shoved her away, discarded her like she didn't matter.

And she, fool that she had been, hadn't used the brains god gave her and allowed him to manipulate her into leaving.

When she knew, she *just knew* that what he wanted, what anyone really wanted was love when we felt most unlovable.

Look what Ishqi had done for her.

Oh, Drake. I'm so sorry.

"I can see I've lost your attention," Jay commented lightly.

Anya shook her head and winced. That too wasn't faked. Her head was still woozy from the sedative. And the cheek bruise. "I...Could I have some water?" She allowed tears to enter her voice. "I feel so faint."

Jay gave her an impatient look. "You're so fucking weak, Anya. I thought you'd put up more of a fight."

Anya swallowed. "Why would you think that?"

"Because of Fallahil, of course. I figured you had to be something special to hold his interest. After all." Jay leaned in and traced her dry and trembling lips with his creepy finger. "You've been fucking him for the last two months, right?"

Anya nodded, slowly. Relieved beyond measure Jay didn't know about the parody of a marriage arrangement she'd had with Drake. "I have. But it meant nothing. Of course. He was just...a means to an end."

Her heart thudded, so slow she felt drugged all over again. But she'd do anything to wipe off that look in Jay's eyes. He looked homicidal at the idea of Drake and her together. It made no sense because she was nobody.

"That sanctimonious motherfucker has been dicking around with us for the last month. He wanted to audit our books before we signed the letter of intent." Jay rose up in an impatient movement.

"I allowed it. I gave him fucking access to whatever records he wanted. And when I thought I had him, when we'd signed the deal that bastard *fucked* me." Jay growled.

"Ho-how?" Anya stuttered.

Jay gave her a bitter look. "He did the same thing to Runwal Realty that we've done to so many of our comps. He undercut every single bid for every single property we were looking to develop for the next five years. And, if that wasn't enough, he made Chan Holdings leverage their position with our bank and call in our credit note."

Anya sucked in a shocked breath. As she tried to sort through the implications of what Jay was saying.

Because, if what he was saying was true, then the letter of intent she'd seen the other night was a hoax. A smokescreen.

A lie Drake had used to lure the Runwals to their ruin.

It meant, he'd *lied* to her. When he'd told her he was an evil, shady bastard…

"He took *everything* from me," Jay spat. "Everything my brother and I worked so hard for all of these years. It takes energy and labor to plan insurance scams too, you know."

"I bet it does," she agreed bitterly. "I bet the people you swindled might feel differently though."

"You know what? You're right."

He bent down and roughly jerked her chin up, staring at her with fresh, murderous hate. "I have been trying to figure something out for the longest time, though. Where did you convince him to fuck you, Anya? It wasn't at Bacchanalia. You were terrified that night, weren't you?"

"The night I tried to find proof against your crimes," Anya reminded him icily.

Jay shrugged. "My brother's computer wouldn't have revealed anything, anyway."

"What do you mean?"

Jay gave her a supremely cocky smile. One that made rage course through her slender body. "It means I am a lot more old-fashioned than my brother when it comes to record-keeping. And that's all I'm going to say, Ms. Mallya-Bhatt. But let's get back to you. And your…"

He tucked one hand over her tee shirt and tore it in half. "Charms."

She shrank away from him, hunching into herself. Hiding herself from his rapacious glance.

"How did you convince Drake to choose you when he wouldn't have Aster Chan on a silver platter?"

Anya laughed. Loud and free. On edge. "I didn't."

"Don't lie. Lying's disrespectful, Anya." Jay slapped her across the mouth. The edge of his ring splitting her lip.

Blood tricked down in a hot rush and Anya saw stars in her head. But she continued laughing. "I'm not lying. I learned that from him," she assured Jay. "I'm not lying."

"You can't tell me you didn't throw yourself at the richest man in this fucking city?"

"I did," she agreed softly. "I very much did. But not that night. I should have." The first tear spurted out of her.

"I should have," she repeated.

Regret and grief rose in a great wave over her. As Jay's words confirmed the truth she'd known deep inside her heart all along.

The thing that had made her not weep, that had forced her to stay awake night after night determined to not think of Drake. Of his stunning eyes, of the gentle strength of his eyes, the power of him…

The thing she'd seen sometimes on his beautiful face when he'd thought she wasn't looking.

Wonder.

"What are you saying?"

"I'm saying," Anya said slowly. Rising up from her crouched position. "That you'll never be able to beat Drake Fallahil. Not ever. He's the best man I know."

Laughter and tears mingled in her heart, burst from her eyes, cleansing her, shaking her…until her broken heart healed from the force of it. Even as it broke anew from the knowledge of never seeing him again.

Not in this life.

Jay's minion butted his gun against her head and she still sat upright. Blood pouring out of a temple wound, her ears ringing again. From pain and hurt.

"That means he's already beaten you."

Jay smacked her across the face. Hard enough that she fell on her side.

Anya spat blood from her mouth. She wondered hazily if this was how Drake felt when he did something terrible to his opponent. When he annihilated them. If so, she wanted to feel this way. Again. And again. Forever.

It was fucking *empowering*.

Anya struggled to sit up because she wanted to face this man, this sniveling coward with all the knowledge of the wrath about to befall him.

"He's won."

Jay screamed obscenities as two people came at Anya. With guns. She put her hands up to shield herself, knowing this was it…This was how it all ended.

She was dying for a good cause.

And he was worth it.

NINETEEN

"I can't find her," Shane ground out, thirty minutes later.

Drake gave him an obsidian stare. "Of course you can find her. What the fuck are you saying?"

Shane shook his head, frustration evident in every line of his tense body. He looked at the computer screen in Drake's office. Running his hands over the keyboard lightly. "I honestly cannot. I accessed the Runwals' apartment camera and it showed Ajay shooting Ishqi Kathuria. Anya's half-sister."

"Damn it."

"A traffic cam near an intersection showed me Anya in a Citroen two blocks from where Ishqi was shot, possibly with surveillance equipment. Its how I found her shoe." Shane and Drake both looked at Anya's shoe.

Such an innocuous looking thing to hold his very sanity, Drake thought dispassionately.

"I'm guessing Ajay can't be in two places if he was shooting Ishqi up in the parking garage of his apartment. He had an accomplice." Drake ran a shaking hand through his wet hair. Water plopped into the collar of his rumpled baby-pink shirt over a nut-brown jacket. The same one he'd worn for two days running. He sweated lightly even though he'd just stepped out of the shower because of the thing he wore under the jacket.

Businessman's Kevlar. Yep, this was why he'd eschewed the need to hire security round-the-clock. Too bad, he'd not thought of giving Anya the same consideration before inviting her to walk away from him…

Fuck.

Mili looked up from where she was working two phones and a laptop. "That would be Jay Runwal." She gave them both a grim look. "I have been checking the records we audited for that fake letter of intent and his signature is on the shady ones. Not Ajay's."

"Jay's the mastermind then?" Shane mused. "That's twisted. Even for him."

Drake narrowed his eyes, even if part of his brain was howling like wild, wounded animal.

Somewhere in this godforsaken city, was his Anya. His brave and courageous Anya. Merciless at the hands of men stronger than her, no matter how leonine her spirit was.

He closed his eyes.

The ghostly specter of Anya being shot by Ajay loomed in his mind. With stunning clarity.

His eyes flew open even as panic gripped him by the throat. Held him immobile for a long, torturous second.

"How can we not find her? What the fuck am I paying you for?" He demanded of Shane.

Shane nodded stiffly, like an old man. "I'm sorry, I failed."

Mili shot them both an impatient look. "We can all play the blame game later. Right now, I need leads to give the cops. So far they have struck out on the penthouse, the raid in the Runwals' office at Marina Bay and the one confirmed safe house we know of."

Drake felt his blood run cold. Maybe it was already too late. Maybe the unthinkable had already happened.

Maybe Anya was already ripped from his life and he didn't even know it. He hadn't even felt it happen.

Then, as it happened when the fear became too much, when it finally had him whole in its wide, uncompromising jaw, his brain, ever the salvation, came to his rescue. Shutting off all other functions, like his newly-awakened heart awash with love. Like the fear, which was a dragon breathing fire into his veins. Burning him from the inside out.

Drake thinking was a monster unleashed.. Deadly, lethal purpose moving through him. Icing him. Protecting him like armor while he prepared to do what he did best.

Win.

~~~~~

"You know the one thing Anya is?" He asked quietly
~~~~~

"What?"

"Sentimental. She's infernally clever but she is even more sentimental," Drake answered promptly.

"What do you mean?" Shane stared at him, thunderstruck. "Fuck. Your fucking watch."

Drake nodded, as blessed calm filled him. Quieting the chaos of grief and terror in him. Because the one thing he was good at was reading people. Knowing them. Exploiting them for his own ends.

Studying Anya was his favorite thing in the world. Learning the many facets of her. So he knew, even though there was no reason for him to hope, he knew she'd still be wearing the watch he'd given her that last luckless day.

She'd do it as a reminder to herself to not trust any man ever again. As a symbol of his perfidy. But she'd do it.

Because Anya was damned sentimental.

Shane swung in the chair and started tapping the keys urgently. He knew exactly what he was doing now. Drake could allow him to conduct this portion of the quest. He wasn't as fast with the keys as Mili and Shane.

No, his real skill lay elsewhere with his hands.

"Did you give your precious watch to Anya?" Mili asked.

Drake nodded, rubbed his hand over his nape. It, too, came back sweaty. Disquiet filled him when he realized he was perspiring everywhere, not just inside his jacket. As if he was nervous. Afraid. "Yeah. I gave it to her the day she…I gave it to her the other day. I revoked communication access when she left but the GPS should still be active on it."

"Why would she still wear it then if you revoked communication access?" Mili wondered.

"Because." Drake smiled. He saw Mili's eyes widen at the gesture and wondered how unhinged he looked. How crazed. If it was even half as crazed as he felt inside it was probably a terrible sight to behold.

"It's exactly the last thing I'd expect her to do and Anya Fallahil lives to defy me."

"Found her." Shane exclaimed. "It's an abandoned lot off Great Albert Street. One of those McMansions which never got made because of too many accidents."

"Accidents the Runwals' engineered," Mili surmised. "I'm calling the cops now." She was already dialing the emergency rescue number.

Drake checked his watch. "The cops will take fifteen minutes. I can be there in seven minutes. If I drive."

Shane held the keys to his Yamaha RZX 200. "Five if I do."

"Let's go."

Mili gave them both a worried glance. She pushed her falling hair back into the bun. Then she nodded, her face quietening. "I'll call the cops. You guys go now."

Drake would have kissed her if he could have spared the energy and time. "I'm gifting you the company of your choice for this, Mils," he vowed.

She gave a watery chuckle. "I'll be happy to get a year-long severance package, boss."

Shane wore his jacket and shook his head at the both of them. "Rich people. I'll never get you lot at all."

"It's very simple, really." Drake followed him out of the office at a fast, purposeful clip. "We keep what's ours."

~~~~~~

Exactly five minutes and thirty seconds, breaking every single speed record there was, Shane and Drake arrived at a hulk of a building. It looked a wreck under the light of the full moon.

Drake clocked the area. It was empty of surveillance cameras, the paved driveway the only part of construction to have survived the Runwals' attempt at scamming the clients and the insurers.

"They'll be ready with firepower," Shane said. He had high-powered night vision binoculars dangling from his neck. "Maybe you should wait here, Mr. Fallahil. You're not equipped to win this war. These are dangerous people."

Drake expertly slid into the hostler tucked into his back. Withdrew a Walther PPK and slid the magazine in with an audible snick. "You can't keep me away from her if you tried, McRae."
~~~~~~

He gave the other man, far more experienced and yet no match for the monster roaring inside him, an imperious look. "So don't try."

Shane gave him a long, thoughtful look. "Alright. Cover my six." They stopped a little away from the door, and Shane extracted a tiny scanner-like thing. It had a square lens attached to the broad head.

Drake watched as he used it to clock the interior of the house and check for heat signatures. He found three.

"Use the gun as a last resort," Shane instructed him tersely as he went over with the portable heat-sig scanner again. "Don't hit anyone intentionally even if your fancy lawyers will get you off with no jail time."

Shane gave him a grim look, extracting a Sig Sauer with a suppressor screwed on. He held it with the ease of long familiarity, of comfort even.

"Try and avoid get killed," he added with a touch of morbid humor. "Ms. Mili and Mrs. Fallahil will murder me if I let it happen on my watch."

They looked at each other for a second then, guns out, entered the enemy's lair.

TWENTY

Drake had never been in a dogfight before. Sure, he'd been in his share of bar brawls with chairs breaking and bottles smashing on someone's head. But those men or women were half in their cups. There was a petty reason for the fight in the first place, and it got broken up in mere moments.

This time was different.

This time, when Drake rounded the half-burnt staircase of the property he was confronted by two men toting Uzis.

He didn't even think. He just butted his head on the nose closest to him, grabbing the other's ones Uzi.

Shane whistled as he dispatched a couple more on the steps ahead with a roundhouse and an uppercut and, for good measure, bashed their heads together.

Drake breathed hard, wiping sweat and blood and bits of nostril matter from his hair and forehead. His head rang like he'd already lost to the champ.

Shane gave him a look behind his back. "You're good, sir?"

"Get up there. Now," Drake growled.

He tucked the gun into his waistband, aware he was taking his life into his hands. Aware, even more that every second he wasted was a second Anya's life was in that worthless piece of shit's hands.

That. Was. Unacceptable.

He pounded up the stairs, his boots taking the punishment of his strides.

Shane was doing most of the heavy lifting with breaking noses and shattering bones with well-placed kicks to the four heavies who met them.

But Drake did his share too. He might not have years of military training and the sense of a field agent taking down enemies with thoughts and words. But he had brute strength and the mightiest weapon of them all.

Fury.

Unholy, possessing fury. The idea of any of these men touching, harming what was *his,* what he'd claimed on a night when he didn't had the good sense to know it, burned bright inside of him. So he took it out on them.

Kicking, punching, roundhouses and uppercuts to jaws, flying men out of his way as much as Shane McRae was.

They went through another round on the next landing and this time, one of the men snuck through his guard. Nicked him with a curved dagger, catching him in the coat. Luckily for him, he was wearing Kevlar under it so the thing stuck in the vest. He twisted the knife inside him, taking the man's wrist with it.

Drake grinned while the man whimpered. "Shouldn't have done that. That's a fucking expensive suit, man."

He kicked the man's legs from under him while he clutched at his broken wrist.

"Go up," Shane shouted. "I'll handle these fucks. You get Anya out. There's no telling what that bastard's done to her."

Drake's fury cooled, iced into a thing of utter destruction.

He nodded and, taking the knife that the man had been kind enough to strike him with, ran up. Taking the steps two and three at a time. Each step felt like a massive leap, an obstacle course where he ran past his own breath, his bones, every single fear he'd ever had.

About losing the person he was unfortunate enough to care about.

But this wasn't about him.

Drake shook his head.

No, this was about rescuing Anya. Everything else could wait.

Even his godforsaken guilt.

He spied a whole door, a thing of beauty actually. Made of cedar wood with carved wooden handles in the shape of a lion. Pretty apropos, if you thought about it. Drake stomped lightly to the landing and took a running leap at the door. He didn't know how many people waited for him inside it.

And he knew the odds of him making it out were slim. But, he'd given the cops time to get here, evened the odds in their favor.

Shane would do the rest.

Drake then did a thing he'd always wanted to do.

He stretched his long leg out, inhaled a mighty breath in and, with a ferocious exhale, smashed the door out of his way.

~ ~ ~ ~ ~

The door splintered into two pieces, the shock of which rang up his legs. Almost crippling him where he stood, his knee absorbing most of the weight of the stupid thing he'd just done.

For a second, there was total silence at his entry.

Then, men started shouting. He heard the sounds of guns being cocked in his direction.

Drake fell down to the ground and started crawling while the bullets came fast and furious at him. Some of them stung the marble of the floor, chips flying in his face, cutting his cheeks, his nose. Some of the heavier pieces fell on his back with the force of an actual bullet.

Still he kept on moving, presenting as little a target as possible to the assailants.

Because he'd seen the only thing he wanted to see in the world.

In the interminable second it had taken everyone to understand what happened, he'd seen the familiar, beloved figure of Anya Mallya-Bhatt. Crouched on the floor, hands bound in front of her. Her mass of curls, the only indication it was indeed her.

But he'd know that hair anywhere. He'd held it wrapped in his hands when he'd loved her so hard it had brought to his eyes, he who never cried.

Tears streamed down his face now, from the dust and the hurt and still he plowed on.

He made it twenty feet before a ring of bullets stopped him cold. They stopped inches from where he was, a circle of death he couldn't possibly cross.

"Alright, alright." He yelled. "I give up."

The ringing stopped. There was total silence once again.

~ ~ ~ ~ ~ ~

Drake smelled the god-awful stench of cordite, metal, and burnt plaster.

He coughed, kept his hands up in the gesture of surrender and slowly straightened to an upright position, one knee on the ground, the other stretched behind him for leverage. But, mostly because it was the bad knee. He wasn't sure it was up to bearing his weight just yet.

The smoke from all the shooting cleared as he blinked.

Finally, he could see his opponent. The motherfucker.

"Jay," he said smoothly. "Nice to see you, man."

Jay grunted. "I'm not thrilled to see you here, Fallahil. What the fuck are you doing here, anyway?"

Drake nodded at the gun. "Well, trying to talk you out of making some spectacularly bad decisions. But, you go ahead. Shoot me if you want to."

Jay shook his head. As if to clear it.

Drake shot one look to Jay's side. Anya lay still there, next to a taller girl in heels. She had purple curls too and wore a leather skirt. Her bleeding hand kept twitching.

Anya was too still. Surely she couldn't be…

"Aah, I see you've found my guests," Jay said as smoothly as Drake had been moments before.

"Is that what you call them?" Drake commented. "I shudder to think what you'd do to people who are your enemies, Jay."

Jay shrugged. "Maybe you're about to find out."

"Maybe. Can I stand up? This knee's gone to shit." Drake gave him a bland smile. The one he always, *always* used in negotiations. Which fooled everyone into thinking Drake was giving them what they wanted.

When he was preparing to move and take everything they ever desired.

But Jay didn't know that. Jay'd only see his weakness because Jay was weak. Cowardly.

"Kicking a door in is bad for the health. Who knew?" Drake smiled wider, knowing he had to keep the man engaged.

Shane would get in any second now. That was their real advantage.

"Yeah. Stand the fuck up. I'd rather shoot you in the head with you standing on your own two feet."

Jay leveled the Uzi square on his forehead and inched him up.

~ ~ ~ ~ ~

Drake groaned, only half in theatrics, as he balanced his weight on his legs. Standing up inch by inch. Now he presented a bigger target to Jay but that was to be expected.

"Are you sure we can't settle this like two businessmen?" He asked reasonably.

He deliberately did not gaze, even peripherally, at Anya. He'd lose all semblance of civility if he did. And there was time yet for him to lose his shit.

"Businessmen?" Jay shot off a round between Drake's feet. Neatly. "For that, I need to be left with a business. Don't I?" He shot off another round. This time near Drake's outstretched hand.

Drake felt something hot spurt out of his hand while the bullet grazed him.

Anya jumped to life.

Drake's heart stopped but he kept Jay focused on him. "You do, Jay. And you still could."

"I could?" Jay's lips twisted in a grimace. "How the fuck could I do that?"

Drake shrugged. Impossible considering he had both hands up in the air, his heart in his mouth, and his fucking palm was bleeding. "I could make all this go away. I just need to make two phone calls. That's it."

Jay stared incredulously, disbelieving at him. "That's it? That's *it*? How about…I make you pay for all the aggravation you caused me? How about that, huh?"

In a lightning fast move Drake couldn't intercept, Jay grabbed Anya by the hair and forced her to her feet. He pointed the gun at her throat. His eyes gleaming manically.

"Should I shoot her? Would that make you happy or sad?"

It'd end him.

"Let the girl go, Jay," Drake said calmly. "You have me. Let her go."

Anya's ravaged face was a flaming sword to his heart. There was blood on both her cheeks, bruises on her temple with a wound bleeding out. And her eyes...she looked so *alive,* as tears streamed down her face.

"Drake," she whispered.

Drake closed his mind, his brain, his heart off to her.

"Drake, he..."

"Shut up!" Jay butted her side with the gun and yanked her head back when she doubled up from the pain.

Drake's heart slowed down. Everything slowed down. He focused with all his might on the only thing that mattered. The sound of footsteps coming up the stairs.

"So, what do you think, Fallahil?" Jay asked.

"Drop the gun, Runwal," Shane yelled as he burst through the door. "Drop the fucking gun."

Jay's concentration was broken, the gun wavered in his hand.

Anya, his brave and courageous and *smart* Anya, did the only thing she could do. She butted Jay's chin, stepped on his instep and dropped to her knees.

Drake did the thing he wanted to. He smiled a terrible monstrous smile. Withdrew the knife he'd been clutching in his palm, making it bloody but not caring anyway.

He walked toward Jay, his bleeding hand outstretched.

Jay tried to squeeze off a round but Drake reached him and he shot the barrel up sky high.

Then he punched Jay, over and over again, holding onto the gun as leverage, so Jay felt the shock ring up twice over. Till his jaw was mush. Then, Drake kicked him in the kidneys so the man doubled over.

Drake took him down and pounded into him, the rage so pure and vicious it poured out of him as heaven's wrath itself.

"You. Don't. Touch. Her. Ever. Again. Again. Again." The words poured out of him till he couldn't see straight, as sweat and saliva and Jay's soft bones mingled in his hands and he became the monster he was always meant to be.

TWENTY-ONE

Anya came to consciousness in a nightmare within the world's best dream.

She saw Drake, well, she saw two of him, since her vision had doubled. But there were two Drakes there, holding his hands up as he rose. His nose bloody, his hair in utter disarray, and his hand…dear god, his hand was bleeding.

She was convinced it was a dream because this Drake wore a rumpled suit. She could see bits of dust and even tears on it.

Her Drake was stupidly fastidious. He had a sartorial sense bar none. He'd never be caught dead without his pocket square!

"You do, Jay," dream Drake said smoothly. "And you still could."

Anya tried to keep her mind, her eyes open but consciousness was still elusive. So she missed the next several moments. Only jerking back to life when a sudden, blinding pain filled her head. Splitting it.

She tried to clutch at it, but felt human skin. Silk suit.

Drake?

No, he'd never hurt her like that. Not in a million years.

Anya opened her eyes again.

Heard the tail end of what Jay was saying. The question he'd asked. "Happy or sad?"

Anya wanted to laugh. Desperately. But she was held too tightly by the madman. Her head hurt, her body hurt. Every inch of her hurt. And Drake…even dream Drake would not look at her.

Was she forever doomed to love unwisely? Love people who'd never need her? Why was she so unlucky?

She was so focused on her own thoughts that she missed whatever it was the dream Drake said. But she didn't miss the look he shot her.

Stay still, it said.

Stay still? As if she'd be able to do that when he was here. When every trembling, tired breath in her body was urging to break free of the madman's hold. And run to her Drake. Because, dream or not, he'd come for her.

He'd come for her. She was important to him. And that was enough. Whatever else happened this was enough for her.

"Drake," she croaked out. Her throat on fire.

Drake flickered her another glance. He looked so different. Not helpless, even though he had his hands up in the air. More…demonic. Because his eyes were blade-sharp.

But Jay Runwal, for that was the madman's name, was more dangerous.

He had a gun.

Anya suddenly remember what she had to tell Drake.

"Drake he…"

Then it was blessed darkness again. For a long moment. Before she was yanked back up brutally, her head, her back, her very skin on fire.

Anya stifled the cry that wanted to tear out of her throat. She tried to scrabble against the hold Jay had on her but couldn't. She hung there, in agony from breathing, from trying to do the right thing…

"Drop the gun, Fallahil," Shane McRae said as he burst into the room too.

Anya blinked. Because even she couldn't dream this elaborately. Shane was in America. He'd not traveled back with them to Singapore, had he? She blinked again, corralling her wavering brain into thinking.

Thinking again.

So she saw Jay's gun pointed away from Drake. The man she loved.

Anya did what her self-defense trainer had told her to do. She heaved against Jay's slippery hold, butting him in the chin with her skull. Her skull rang from the impact while she squashed his instep with her naked foot, grinding into it with all her might.

And, for good measure, she ducked down when she felt him clutching at her. Painfully. Furiously.

And then… then Anya witnessed the most terrifying and beautiful thing of all.

She saw her Drake, her beloved, smile like the wrath of the devil possessed him. The blue of his eyes glowing in unholy glee, a second before he started walking. Almost in slow motion.

She saw him take on the madman, his hand outstretched while blood dripped down his hand.

She saw Drake shoot the gun up to the ceiling so plaster rained down like snowflakes around them.

And she saw, with jerky breaths, as Drake punched Jay over and over and over again. Holding the gun as leverage.

Kicking him in the gut and when Jay went down, Drake followed him, sitting on his chest, pounding on him over and over. The sound of bone and flesh sickening, gut-wrenching.

Anya swayed because she wanted to breathe. And she wanted, desperately, to touch Drake. Even this demonic Drake.

But she was afraid it would be a dream and the dream would end.

So, she slumped on the ground, even as tears poured out of her, and fell to her side.

Anya closed her eyes. The sight of him beating the life out of Jay Runwal the last thing she wanted to see.

But also the only thing.

~~~~~~

The next time Anya opened her eyes, she was blinded. Again.

She blinked rapidly, her heart thudding rapidly. And felt the steady, comforting beat of her own heart beeping out of a monitor.

She breathed shallowly, tried to ground herself in her surroundings. Fact one, she was in a hospital. Fact two, this meant she wasn't dead. Fact there, this definitely meant Ishqi was shot and Drake had…

Her heartbeat jacked up again.

Anya sat bolt upright.

"Hey, hey, sis." Ishqi patted her shoulders.

Anya's breath came out in gasps and she clutched at Ishqi's good wrist. The other one was taped her to her side in a medical sling.

"You're okay? You're okay, Ishqi?"

Ishqi nodded, tears filling her unpainted yes. "I'm fine. I'm *fine*, Anya. The bullet went through and through. It didn't hit any vital organs so I just have this bitch of a
~~~~~~

scar." She gave a watery smile. "And all the happy pills I could ever want."

Then her smile vanished. "But it's you we were worried about. You didn't wake up for a whole day."

"Oh." Anya gulped. "Was I like in a coma or something?"

Ishqi shook her head. "No. The doctors said you were sleeping naturally. Apparently you've been sleep-deprived for a few days now. So your body was getting its rest. Finally."

Anya chuckled. It sounded weak even to her own ears. "Nothing like getting kidnapped and beaten up for the body to get some rest, right?"

Isqhi sat down in a thump next to her. "Don't even *joke* about that, Anya. Mom hasn't stopped crying since Drake called her." Ishqi laid her head on Anya's aching shoulder, even as her heart jerked at Drake's name. "She blames herself for both her daughters trying to act like they're superheroes and take down the bad guys."

Anya chuckled as she put a hand around Ishqi's waist. "Did we, though? Take down the bad guys?"

Ishqi nodded.

~~~~~

Right then, the opened door admitted the perky and pretty form of Mili. Who looked distinctly un-perky and un-pretty in her rumpled clothes. Her tired smile was broad and heartfelt.
~~~~~

"You two did not just take down the bad guys. You took them behind the school shed and schooled them. Ajay's in custody at Changi airport after shooting you, Ishqi and Jay's…" Mili shuddered delicately. "He's going to need reconstructive surgery when he wakes up."

Anya flashed to Drake whaling on Jay, systematically. Methodically. That couldn't have possibly happened.

"Anyway," Mili continued, "I've talked the police chief down to giving you a commendation and no media interviews."

Mili kissed Anya's forehead. "You can consider it my thank you for being such a shitty friend all these days, Anya."

Anya squeezed Mili's hand. Tight.

"Thank you," she spoke in a heartfelt tone. "For everything, Mili."

Ishqi instantly went on the defensive. "Don't call my sister shitty, woman."

Mili gave her a considerably cooler look. "I've also asked the authorities to extend their courtesy to you and expunge your records of any past legal infractions." She paused for a glacial second. "You're welcome, Ms. Kathuria."

Ishqi subsided with a muttered thanks. She hopped off the bed and gave her sister a searching glance. "Is it cool if I leave you, babe? Do you need anything?"

"No, honey. I'm fine." Ishqi nodded to the both of them and exited the hospital room, her head bent over her phone already.

"The doctor's coming to see you in a minute," Mili said quickly to Anya. "Now's the time to get to the loo. I could help you if you need it."

Anya did a quick inventory of her own body. Yes, it pained and creaked like she was in her eighties. But nothing seemed broken or even bruised. She moved her jaw.

Ouch. She'd spoken too soon.

Anya slid off the bed. "Nah. I'm good, Mils. Can you wait for me outside? I'll get done with the doctor's examination and then we can talk properly." She gave her a wan smile. "I can apologize for being a shitty friend. At length."

"I expect several bottles of wine. Good wine. As a thank you."

"Done." Anya was about to turn and leave when she couldn't help it. She asked the question burning on her tongue. "Where's he, Mili? Where's Drake?"

Mili looked like she was about to say something. But she only brushed Anya's hair back and said, "Loo now. Everything else can wait, right?"

Anya nodded miserably. Because she knew Mili had the bad habit of telling the truth like her employee. And if she wasn't answering, it is because she wanted to avoid the question.

Ergo, Drake wasn't here.

"Sure," she said firmly. "Thanks, babe."

~ ~ ~ ~ ~

Anya took several deep, stitch-filled breaths as she did her business. Imitating sleeping beauty was hell on the bladder and gut. When she was done, she felt marginally better, although a part of her was still so resigned to the hurt.

The man had come to save her like the devil himself and then not bothered to stick around and see if she was okay.

Typical.

Blessed, energizing anger took the place of lethargic melancholy and Anya perked up. Just because he hadn't deigned to come check on her didn't mean she had the same ego problems.

No, first thing when she was sprung out of here, she was going to go find him and give him a fucking piece of her..

Anya yanked the bathroom door open and found Drake there, bandaged hand raised to knock.

TWENTY-TWO

He stared at her with burning eyes. His face bruised with little nicks on his nose, his cheeks. He wore the same suit. *Still.*

"You shouldn't be out of bed," he rumbled. "Didn't the doctor prescribe bed rest for you?

"What do you care what the doctor told me?"

He let out a shaky breath that turned the whites of his eyes red with unshed tears. "I care about you, Anya. I care only about you."

"Then, you have a lot to answer for." She poked at his chest with a shaking hand.

He stumbled back. Another first. "Anya…"

"No," she shook her head first. Riding the edge of the anger flickering to life. "No, me first. Why did you not tell me what your plan was with Runwal, in the first place?"

"That's what you want to talk to me about?" His eyes searched her face. Tracking all over her as if he couldn't believe them. As if she was…wonderful.

"Yes," she snapped. Not allowing herself a second of hope. Because the last time had nearly killed her and she wasn't willing to do that to herself again. "Yes, damn you. We talk business. It's your favorite language, isn't it?"

His lips twitched. She had the insane idea he wanted to smile at her.

"My favorite language is the one you want to speak," Drake said quietly.

"I don't believe you. Tell me about the Runwals," she spoke sharply.

"They're done bothering you. Or anyone. I guess Mili gave you the rundown on how we caught Ajay when he was trying to flee to Dubai. And Jay's should be in surgery, momentarily."

"Yeah, after you half-killed him with your bare hands," she shot back. "Who pulled you back from him, by the way?"

"Mili did, when she arrived with the police. And, I'd have killed Jay whole for daring to touch you," Drake said softly. Openly. His heart in his eyes. There for her to see if she was brave enough to look.

Anya's eyes rounded. Her breath hitched because hope, that insidious, stubborn demon reared its head under her breast. Right in her heart. "You don't mean that. You couldn't mean that after what you said to me the other day."

"I was planning to put the Runwals out of commission since LA. Shane was working on leverage for me. You and your sister arrived at it from a different angle and in far less time than I, I should add." He sounded frankly impressed.

"Shane's another thing I wanted to talk about. How did he come….there?"

"Shane's been following you," he said bluntly. "I couldn't leave you completely unprotected while the Runwals still ran amok."

Anya stared at him like he'd grown horns.

"Although, it wasn't enough and I can never forgive myself for what happened. I'm so sorry, sweetheart. I'm so *sorry*." He took another shaky breath. This one looked painful and Anya realized he looked like he'd gone ten rounds with three champs and lost.

She didn't want to unbend toward him for being remorseful and chivalrous in his own fucked up way, so she latched onto the flaw in his grand plan.

"Unbelievable," she muttered. "So you sicced a bodyguard on me without telling me and came to save me from the bad guy to prove what, Drake? That I'm silly and stupid? That I need your help? What was the point of all this?"

She sat down on the bed. Staring at her bandaged hands. Feeling so many other things coursing through her now that the rough edge of the anger was burning itself out. She felt spent.

"The point, Anya, is I love you," Drake said quietly.

Anya's head swam with tears. Stupid, weak tears. She put a hand to the side of her temple. Because she was now hearing things.

She blinked. The tears dripped down.

Drake took one of her hands in both of his. The rough bandage abrading her soft skin. The sorriest part of it all was that her pulse still tripped at his touch. It still hungered for him.

She looked up at him through blurry eyes. Saw his face. It was flayed open with all that he felt written on his chiseled face.

The truth shone in of the burning brilliance of his eyes.

Anya gulped.

~ ~ ~ ~

"Finally got you to shut up, didn't I?" Drake went down on one knee. "Good."

"What are you doing? Get up," Anya said, bewildered.

He shook his head. As feeling returned inch by inch into his battered body. Since the second he'd seen her moving. All kinds of magnificent fury lining her pretty face. And her eyes, those pretty eyes were right there, giving him the clues he needed. To talk to her.

Tell her how he felt.

Confess.

"Not yet. I have a lot to apologize for. And someone once told me apologies are best given on bended knee." He winced as the bad knee trembled. "Although I might have to get up in a hot minute."

"Why?" she sniffed. "I thought you had a lot to apologize for."

But she left her hand in his and he took that to be an encouraging sign.

"I kicked the door down to get to you. Banged up my knee pretty bad."

"You kicked the…" Her jaw dropped. "That was the stupidest thing to do."

"Yes," he admitted readily. "That was the second stupidest…no third stupidest thing actually."

"Oh, you're actually admitting to being stupid? The great and infallible Drake Fallahil?" She tried to tug her hand away and he thought, for a moment, that he could do it.

Give her the space she needed. Let her come to him. He could be that noble and heroic.

Drake held on tighter, unable to let go.

"The second-stupidest thing was blackmailing you into marrying me in that farce of a ceremony. When the adult thing to do, like my therapist and Mili told me, was to simply ask you out. I like you, Anya. Will you go out with me?"

"Your therapist." Anya shook her head. "I'm dreaming. This is a dream. You can't be going to therapy."

"I tell you I like you and you're talking about my therpay?" This time he smiled.

Anya searched his face, frankly gazing down at him.

As he stared at her beloved face, he felt the familiar need to shield himself. It was ever-present. An itch under his skin. As if the world was a cruel thing out to hurt him the second he presented his vulnerable side.

But this wasn't the world. This was his Anya.

And she'd never once turned him away. She'd never once hurt him when he didn't deserve it.

"I go to therapy every day now," he found himself saying. Trapped into confessing the truth when she looked at him like that. Like she could begin to believe in him again. "I have control issues. Trust issues. Abandonment issues. And I avoid it all by using copious amounts of work as an excuse to not do the inner work."

"Right." She nodded.

"So yeah. I mean…I go to therapy because I'd like to…"

"Do the inner work?"

Drake shook his head. "Become worthy of telling you how I feel about you."

Anya sighed. "I think you made it abundantly clear how you feel about me, Drake. I don't want to…"

"I love you," he said quickly.

She swallowed. He saw the movement in the vulnerable column of her throat. And said it a third time.

"I love you, Anya."

~ ~ ~ ~ ~

Anya gave him a hurt look. It was filled with so much recrimination his heart hurt all over again. At the idea that he could have done this to her. Made her feel like this.

"I'm so sorry. I'm so *sorry,*" he emphasized. "I've been unconscionable with you. I know that. Even without the therapy I knew that. So I tried to set you free the other day. The Runwal deal was just an excuse to do that."

"You weren't setting me free," she said simply. "You were pushing me away to punish yourself."

He nodded, holding her gaze. "I was. That's what the therapy and Mili made me see."

"Bully for you."

"Anya, can you ever forgive me?" He asked softly.

Drake let go of her hands. Wanting, needing her to make the choice. Free and clear of all claim, all past history. All the things they'd been to each other. But knowing it wasn't a huge possibility.

Anya sighed. "Of course, I forgive you. You know I forgive you. You kicked down a door to save my sister and me." Then, she touched his bandaged hand of her own volition. Her bruised and dirty fingers, trembling. "Does it hurt very badly?"

He shook his head. "Nothing hurts like you do, Anya."

She pressed her lips together. "I can't be a weapon you punish yourself with, Drake. I won't be. It'll make me a monster like you. And I'm not a monster."

"I know," he agreed fervently. "I know that now."

He pulled out a sheaf of papers from behind his pants' waistband. The gun clattered to the floor.

He gave her a sheepish grin when she gave him a hard look. "I didn't use it even once. I promise."

"Fine." She leaned back and eyed the papers warily. "What's this, then?"

"These are divorce papers. And the original NDA waiver we signed, null and void now."

She took them in her hands. Crushed them between her fingers. "You want me to sign them?"

He nodded solemnly. "I do. These papers represent my claim on you. And I don't want that anymore."

"Then what do you want?"

"I..." He wet his lips because he didn't know how to articulate the things he felt. The things he wanted.

Needed from this one woman. This woman he'd somehow stumbled into and met like the world's best possible cosmic joke.

"You can't even tell me what you want," Anya muttered tearfully. "How are you ever going to--?"

"I want to take you out to dinner. Somewhere local," Drake began quickly. "Paris or Bora Bora can wait when we get to know each other. Better. Like a real couple. I'll ask you about your school assignments and you can hear me bitch about government red tape in setting up Verdant. But not too much bitching," he added, "because I'm cutting back on work.

"I want to wait three dates to kiss you while I imagine kissing you for each and every one of those dates. I want…"

Anya's eyes grew enormous. She sucked in air through her cheeks. She even clutched his hand, her nails digging into his bandage.

"After a reasonable amount of time, I'll get down on one knee like this." He indicated his current position. "And I'll present you with a free trade sapphire ring to match the necklace some other idiot dumb enough to let you get away gifted you. And I'll tell you, Anya Mallya-Bhatt, you're smart. You know I always tell the truth."

She swallowed and tried to wipe away tears. She also slid down to her knees so they were almost, almost wrapped in an embrace together.

"And what's the truth?"

Drake placed shaking hands on her waist. And held on. Just held on to his whole world. "I don't know if you were made for me or what possessed me to think I could claim the best person I know, for myself. Even though I'm apparently super-smart and I make impossible deals that change the way industries are run. What I do know is this."

This was the easy part. "You've changed the way I run, Anya. You're ten times smarter than me and the possibility of you…it's better than any deal I could ever make. And I'd like to spend the rest of my life proving I was worthy of you claiming me back. If you'll have me."

Anya sniffed loudly.

And Drake wasn't ashamed when her lovely face blurred in front of him because his eyes welled up. He sniffed too. His heart expanded to twice its size. To encompass the whole freaking world.

That was the thing about love. It blew up every single notion you had about yourself. Upended it. Changed you until you were unrecognizable to yourself.

It made all the pain and suffering worth it.

"All my life I thought I was unworthy of love, of being a better man, because of who birthed me and who raised me. You showed me that was the biggest lie of all, Anya."

She cupped his chin and drew him forward. "Shut up and kiss me, you idiot."

"Say yes and I'll kiss you every day for the rest of our lives."

"Yes." Anya almost leaped into his arms, knocking him with her knees against his side.

He almost howled, unmanned by her enthusiasm. But held on for dear life. Racing his hands over her hospital gown, tracing the curves and shape of her. So beloved, so missed!

"YES!" She raced kisses all over his face, his neck, the patch of skin at his throat she adored.

His tears and hers mingling with their soft, wondering laughs.

"Yes, of course, yes. I was planning to leave the country to get over you, you *idiot.*"

"I'd have found you anywhere on earth," he vowed solemnly. "I'm not usually this stupid, you know."

Anya sobbed. "No. You're the smartest, brightest, best man I know."

"I know," Drake framed her face in his hands. "I know that now. I believe you, love."

"That's all I wanted for you, Drake," she said softly. "That you see yourself how I see you. That you love yourself like I love you."

And he saw the way she looked at him. As if he was good, and decent, as if he was a hero. And for her, because of her, he knew he could become one. He didn't have to be like the ones who made him.

Or the ones he worked with.

He was his own man.

He kissed her softly then. With lips and teeth and tongue. Tasting years of loneliness, regret and denial. Tasting the gentle benediction of love returned. Which made it twice as special, beautiful.

Giving back all of himself to her. Giving her the bitterness, the sadness, the aloneness. Giving her the joy, the incandescence, the sheer brilliance of this moment.

He gave her his heart.

And, since Caleb Drake Fallahil always told the truth, he kissed her exactly like this every day.

For the rest of their lives. Their long, happy, filled with laughter and passion and fights lives.

The monster became a better man for love. And never regretted a moment of it.

TWENTY-THREE

A few weeks later…

Ishqi thought she was being followed but wasn't sure. She turned around quickly, her braids almost giving her whiplash when she did so. Found a cos-play couple dressed as Princess Mononoke. They were munching on the chicken shashlik one of the stalls at Hong Lim Market and Food Center, licking the bamboo sticks which pierced the barbequed chicken pieces.

Nope. *Paranoid much, babe,* she thought cynically.

Ishqi munched on the succulent candy jelly she adored and continued strolling through the busiest center of the market. It was an open courtyard, spreading a clear mile in all directions and filled with the aromas of the most delicious meats, veggies and spices being cooked to perfection. Even the most hardened of palettes would find satisfaction in here. And Ishqi was a bonafide food hound.

She quickly spotted the particular vendor, selling the best green tea latte frappes in all of Singapore. He was perched behind a tiny booth, barely enough to contain an industrial size freezer, his huge-ass blender, and a glass display of the different flavors of drinks. A line, consisting of twenty people, snaked from the vendor.

Ishqi joined the throng of people waiting to place their orders, her good hand in the pocket of her boy shorts. The other one was still in a barely there sling, which was now beginning to chafe at the shoulders. After four weeks of light physical therapy, applying antibacterial lotion, and terrible quickie showers she was ready to gain full range of motion and start working again.

Start living again.

"Love the hair, sweetheart," a low, husky voice commented in her ear.

Ishqi started to turn around, excitement churning her belly, but the person tapped her shoulder.

"Keep looking straight ahead." The person sifted through strands of her uncolored hair, returning back to a depressing brown. "Love the shampoo too."

"Yeah, I'm using Anya's stash now. She might have been a tight-ass but hair care is a religion with her."

"I bet." The chuckle tightened her belly and her pussy to painful.

Ishqi moved her hand till it found the person's hand and twined their fingers together. A sting from a pointed ring only made her feel all the more. "I missed you."

"Me too. But the wait's been worth it, hasn't it?"

"It has." Ishqi nodded.

"So, do you have it? Are you going to make me beg for it?"

Ishqi drove her thumb in the middle of the person's index finger, in and out, in and out. Her accomplice clutched harder at her hand. "I'd like to," she commented lightly.

She took the sweet out of her mouth, slipping the tiny thumb drive hidden under her tongue along with it. She rubbed the tiny plastic casing clean of her spit and, for good measure, used an antibacterial wipe to clean it. Then, she palmed it off to her accomplice who sighed in what could only be appreciation.

"Damn, baby. Why would you hide this on your tongue?"

"Because I was shot a month ago for trying to do the right thing and incriminate white collar criminals?" Ishqi suggested sweetly.

Then she turned around and nailed the person with a somber look. "Mostly because I'm sure my brother-in-law has sicced a body on me. He doesn't trust me."

It was really inconvenient that Anya hadn't done the decent thing and broken up with the fucking billionaire. Drake's security measures were scary in the extreme, mostly because they were so damn insidious. He'd apparently invested in a company that chipped you like a heifer and monitored your movements through a, get this, biodegradable satellite which would dissolve in space into nothing!

"You turned around," her accomplice murmured.

"The better to look at you, baby." Ishqi blew a kiss. "Fuck, I missed you."

She leaned in and pulled her accomplice closer by the back pockets. Then she kissed, with tongue. Snaking it inside so the taste of her devil's candy was coated all over her accomplice. Desire made her giddy when she felt the tongue ring scrape slightly over her nerve endings. Her wet pussy remembered what it was like to feel that scrape inside. Intimately.

When they parted, she smiled lightly. A real, vulnerable smile.

"I didn't think we'd do that again."

"We're going to do everything, love. With this, we are set for life." Her accomplice held up the plastic case with the thumb drive. "Jay Runwal was dumb to share critical info with you, wasn't he?"

"Cocky is the word I'd use." Ishqi tapped at her chest. "He didn't think a chick would have the balls to pull off the ultimate heist."

"So, getting shot was part of your plan? Genius."

The line had moved fast while they talked and kissed and they were almost at the counter.

Ishqi stuck her tongue out. "Don't be mean. I did get shot, you know."

"So, you did. And all for a good cause."

"Eight million worth of a good cause," Ishqi reminded. "Did you have any trouble with your end of the arrangement?"

"Nope. The servers are being stood up in a farm in Kansas, awaiting payment. And I hired out the onion routing for running the website." Onion routing was a complicated way of sending information through multiple nodes or ISPs each of which could only be accessed through a verified passcode combination, generated randomly on a keypass possessed by the team conducting the routing.

It was a simple and unverifiable way of dispersing information through the ether web.

Her accomplice tucked the plastic casing in a silver sling bag, almost identical to Ishqi's. They'd gotten the bags together after a job in Bangkok where they'd helped a Thai drug lord launder his money through a dry cleaning outfit and send the profits to the Cayman Islands.

"Filthy Rich Vice will be officially up and running in forty-eight hours. And we'll be officially safe from DDOS, malware, spyware and ransom-ware attacks like Toast of the Town wasn't."

Ishqi smiled grimly. "And everyone will come after us. Won't they?"

"Will your brother-in-law be one of them?"

Ishqi shook her head. "No, I don't think Drake's our target anymore. He's…well, boring now." She made a face. "He takes my sister out on dates even though they are married. Whatever the fuck that means."

"It means whatever the fuck they want it to mean, babe."

"I know." She shrugged. "I just…" Ishqi couldn't explain the peculiar combination of hope and envy she felt every time she FaceTimed with her sister, currently holding meetings in New Delhi, India to set up a four trillion venture capital fund designed to change the world. And save it with the man she loved by her side.

"We're almost at the counter. I'll slip out and get you some food. Ramen?"

Ishqi smiled, as a different sort of fire spread low in her belly. One of warmth and comfort and affection. "You know me so well. Yes, please."

Her accomplice kissed her on the cheek and left in a rustle of air.

Ishqi turned around and placed her order. Green tea latte frappe with skim milk and a blueberry crush smoothie for her accomplice. She swiped her phone, burner, of course, and paid for the drinks.

"I suspected you to be an espresso shot frappe kind of girl, Ms. Kathuria," a low husky voice commented near her ear.

Ishqi sucked in a quick breath as her stomach pitched inside her and fear tightened her insides. She turned around slowly, on one heel.

"Mili Iyer," Ishqi murmured. "How did you find me?"

TWENTY-FOUR

Mili

"You're hard to track Ishqi," Mili replied. She gave the young hacker a smile she hoped came off as hard. "But not impossible."

Ishqi quirked a brow up. "Or you're exceptionally good at your job."

Mili considered telling her she'd quit from the best, the *only* job she'd had for the last decade. But stopped. Ishqi was smart, she'd know this about Mili already. She just wanted to provoke her into a reaction and distract her from her mission.

"Then you know why I'm here."

Ishqi shrugged. Slurped some of the green tea in through a steel straw. "Maybe I do. Maybe I don't."

Mili expelled an exasperated sigh. "How does Anya put up with your brattiness?"

"Got you." Ishqi grinned. "Didn't I?"

Mili's lips twitched of their own volition. Score one for Ishqi. "You did indeed."

"Indeed," Ishqi mimicked her perfectly. "Tell me, does Oxford also do an Upper Crust Accent course or just your regular social sciences degree?"

Mili kept her consternation off her face with effort. Ishqi really had done her homework on Mili. It was disconcerting to say the least. Not to mention, highly invasive. "They call them Masters at Oxford. But then you already know that."

Ishqi shrugged. "Academia bores me. I just don't understand why someone with your brain would want to spend six years of your life studying to become great under some *man* to when you're already great."

Mili thought back to her years of education at two of the best schools money and privilege could buy – Oxford and Harvard. And decided Ishqi was right. The pompousness of some of the professors or dons as Oxford preferred to call its faculty was legendary. Their knowledge and expertise was even more so.

"Didn't it break your feminist little heart to have to say yes sir, no sir to those idiots?" Ishqi pressed.

Mili shook her head. "You're being difficult, Isqhi. But I have your number."

"You do?"

Mili nodded. Played her trump card. "You actually love your sister. So all this posturing is for my benefit and maybe my ex-boss's. Am I right?"

Ishqi shrugged, unconcerned.

But Mili was good at her job. So she could slight tensing of Ishqi's fingers on the frappe cup. Score one for Mili.

"Am I, Ishqi?"

Ishqi glared at her, looking, for the first time like a vulnerable woman. Even though she was just two years younger than Mili. Although, some days, Mili felt a hundred. Especially after she'd spoken to her mama.

"Fine. I know why you're here. It's the money, right?"

Mili shook her head. "I know you know where the money is, Kathuria. Give me some credit," she said wearily.

Ishqi was surprised. It showed in the widening of her eyes, the flare of her nostril. That was unexpected. "How…"

"You're good," she commented. "I guess your partner was right and you did get shot deliberately so Jay Runwal would lead you to the hidden money."

Ishqi pursed her blowup doll lips, her eyes flashing.

Mili could see the fuck you forming on her lips but beat her to it with a smooth, "Where were the files containing all the transactions, then? In another condemned property?"

"In an old abandoned property on Sentosa," Ishqi muttered. "Once Jay said the evidence was somewhere physical all I had to do was follow his trail of destruction.

This property has been untouched for the last decade. About the time they started their little scam."

"You did excellent work helping bring them down, you know. And, for what it's worth," she added softly, "I'm sorry I made fun of your shooting right now."

Ishqi gave her a bitter look. "Are you going to give me a big speech about how I need to return the money and absolve myself of all my sins?" She gave a tiny but pregnant pause. "Does my sister and her filthy rich husband?"

Mili shook her head. "No, Ishqi. I'm not here in an official capacity at all. You know I quit my job three weeks ago. So you can do whatever you want with that money. Although I hope you put the money you've…siphoned to good fucking use. And leave Drake and Anya alone."

Ishqi gave her a disbelieving stare. "You don't think I'll use my own sister as gossip fodder. Not when she doesn't deserve it."

Mili smiled. "I'm glad to know there are some lines still left for you to cross."

Isqhi finished her frappe noisily. "So why *are* you here, then? If not for the money."

Mili hesitated. Wondered how in hell she could frame her request so it did not look like what it was. Breaking international law.

"You need my help," Ishqi surmised. "You need my particular brand of help."

The word 'yes' stuck in Mili's throat. Which was suddenly too tight for her to swallow. She fiddled with the bronze bracelet she'd worn as protection and for much-needed courage.

I am so lost, Mili. Who am I? She heard those words echo in her head again. On an endless loop of shame and guilt. Followed by a wave of helplessness.

Mili straightened her back. "Yes, I do, Ishqi. I need help."

"With what?"

"Finding someone."

Ishqi smiled. "Finding someone where?"

"That's the thing. I don't know where they are," Mili admitted. "All I have is their name."

"And that would be?" Ishqi prompted, softly. With no judgment at all.

Mili felt a rush of gratitude at the woman's gentle question. If she'd gloated, even a little, Mili would have never been able to forgive herself for what she was about to do. Invade someone else's privacy, their very life…with no regard to the cost to be paid. Just because she had made a deathbed promise.

"Mili?"

Mili sighed. Then said the name that had recently begun to haunt her days and nights. "Bhatnagar. Krishna Bhatnagar."

Ishqi's eyes rounded. "Isn't he…?"

"Yes." Mili nodded. "He is the F1 racer, Nihaal Bhatnagar's, father."

Ishqi nodded slowly back. "I see."

Mili knew she didn't. But she appreciated the solidarity. "So, you'll do it? You'll find Krishna Bhatnagar?"

Ishqi reached over and squeezed Mili's wrist, right where the bracelet was stuck to her clammy skin. "If I'm on the trail, Mili, the man is as good as found." She even gave Mili a kindly smile to go with it. One meant to reassure Mili.

Except, it did nothing of the sort inside Mili. It just created more dread to add to the mix of horror, shame and guilt she carried now. One she'd not shared even with Drake, her big brother in all but name…

"Thanks. I'll be reachable on this number when you do."

Ishqi took the card Mili offered, pulled Mili forward in the same motion and gave her a hard kiss on her surprised lips. Mili drew a sharp breath.

"I always wanted to kiss a tall girl," Ishqi explained, dropping down to her toes. "Wonder if you tasted different."

"Do I?" Mili was intrigued and not in the least bit offended.

Ishqi grinned. "Yep. And in the best way possible."

"Thank you," Mili grinned. Feeling loads better than she had since she'd seen Ishqi at the food court, and known she was going to have to buckle down and ask her help in locating a man who had destroyed her life as she knew it. "Sincerely."

"I know." Ishqi pointed at Mili. "So what are you going to do now that you're not working for the most powerful man in Singapore? Retire on your savings?"

Mili shook her head. "I haven't decided yet. But maybe I'll start practicing law again. I miss it."

"Where?"

Wherever Krishna Bhatnagar is. Mili shrugged. "No idea. I'm just taking the time to regroup and relax."

"Okay."

But Ishqi didn't sound like she believed Mili.

Ishqi's phone buzzed. "I have to take this." She thumbed it open.

"You do that," Mili murmured. "When can I expect to hear from you?"

"Soon," Ishqi promised. "I'm giving you the friends and family discount."

"I appreciate it."

Then Mili watched Ishqi plunge into the crowd and merge into it, while she stood in the center of it all. A tall, strong, independent, *seriously* well-dressed woman crumbling on the inside…

One Year Later

There was only one way to describe him. *Fucking naked.*

Mili's heart pounded a jungle drum in her ears while she stared at the expanse of outrageously toned, exquisitely perfect, mouthwatering flanks of Formula One racing's golden boy. His thighs were sculpted things of hard marble sewn with honey brown skin that flexed each time the water hit his striated back. And his buttocks were perfect moons of hardness and flesh. *Delicious.*

He was whistling tunelessly as he showered in the glass cubicle of the hotel bathroom, the door carelessly flung open. So anyone, *her*, could wander inside and get an arresting eyeful.

Don't look down, Mili.

Mili looked down. Spit dried in her throat when she saw the outrageously, perfectly beautiful specimen between his legs. And had the most explicit vision of what it would be like if she went inside right now, got down on her knees and took it in her mouth, the warm water of the shower cascading around them both.

Wet warmth rushed between her legs. Tightening the skin under the loose pants and lacy shell cinched at the waist y a handtooled faux leather belt. Slicking her core against the silk of her Cosabella thongs, while her nipples peaked against the matching silk of her bra.

She drew another sharp breath. As excitement and anger filled her veins.

What the fuck was she thinking? Mili Iyer did not kneel for anyone. Certainly not a man. Not even a man as sexy and perfectly built as this one.

She shook her head once. Took a deep breath to calm her pulsing heart and to bring forth the legendary cool she was known for, globally. The cool she'd won by being assistant to Drake Fallahil, a man who'd made his billions with nothing more than his sharp wit and his sharper brain. She'd assisted him in building his empire while studying for her undergraduate and graduate degrees *and* law, later on.

So a naked man should not derail her determination or her equilibrium.

Then again, she wasn't determined or calibrated equally. Not anymore. Not since the last year.

So, here she was. Flustered and aroused and *aware* of this man singing horribly in his bathroom. While she skulked outside it like some lovestruck groupie. God, she was pathetic.

And it wouldn't do. She'd come here for a job. She needed to do it. Then get the hell out before her head exploded with lust or something far worse. *Shame.* At being caught in such a humiliating position.

Unfortunately, for Mili, fate stepped in like the bitch she was.

Mili took a step forward just as Nihaal Bhatnagar turned in the shower.

Heat rushed through her, suffusing her being. Just as the wet had filled her insides moments ago.

Nihaal's beautifully chiseled face froze in mid-tune. His Adam's apple bobbed up and down but no sound came out. Water poured down his truly athletic physique, delineating each set of muscle and bones.

"I'm sorry," Mili said politely. "For barging in."

To his immense credit, the racer did nothing more than nod at her. He did not cover himself or look enraged at this gross invasion of his privacy. He just stood there, with water falling on him. A god in his prime.

"Why?" Nihaal asked.

Like silk. Like dark desires and whispered promises best broken. His voice, the cadence and accent of it, was more tempting than his body.

"Because I'm here to deliver extremely awful news, Mr. Bhatnagar."

Nihaal cocked his head.

The width of the room stood between them. A healthy hundred feet. But she felt the force of his dark eyes directly on her face. On her very skin. As if a freaking spotlight had landed on her, magnifying her for him alone.

"Yes?"

"I'm sorry," she said again, in a voice rusty with discomfort. "Your father's dead."

"I beg your pardon?" Nihaal asked coolly. But he was naked and there was no way to hide the clench of his fists and the tautening of his stance. "What did you just say?"

His defensiveness erased her discomfort. Made her bolder. Stand up taller. Gave heft and gravity to her words. "Your father, Krishna Bhatnagar, owner of Bhatnagar Champion and Stud Farm, is dead." And then, because it was best to deliver all the bad news at once, she plunged on. "You'll have to come home. To The Homestead. In Kolkata. To take care of his last rites since you're his son and heir."

Then, Nihaal did the least expected thing of all.

He looked her straight in the eye. And laughed.

Mili knew, right then, that her mission had turned from difficult to impossible. And there was nothing she could do about it.

EPILOGUE

Five years later...

"...And the last team to qualify for position is the first-ever carbon neutral team in the history of Formula One Racing, Menzo Monadnock, with Bhatnagar and Alonso. Will we see a similar upset from Bhatnagar that we saw three years ago when he won his first World Championship, beating Verstappen and Hamilton to the podium?"

Drake leaned forward from the comfy wing chair he'd claimed for the duration of the race. Since it was the chair closest to the TV screen. "Win, damn you, Nihaal," he muttered. "You better win. I don't care how badly you timed in Practice. You still got this."

The cars purred into action in their respective positions, sleek and terrible beasts with unimaginable horsepower – death traps in the making. The forty-inch TV screen did no justice to the power and majesty of the machines competing for pole position at the Singapore Grand Prix. And, if this had been any other time, Drake would have been in the Menzo pit, protecting his investment.

Although, truth be told, co-owning an F1 racing team had less to do with money and more to do with his own desire to race a bullet-fast machine. Not that anyone allowed him into the caboose of the twenty-five million dollar carbon-neutral racing prototype. And here he was, unable to see his precious investment in action, up close and personal.

"Crap," Drake looked at the race position.

Nihaal was sandwiched between Verstappen and Luiso, a new kid on the block who was blowing past everyone's lap times, one by one. Including the late and legendary Ayrton Senna. Menzo's head was making noises about inviting the ingénue to Menzo's stable. And Drake and the other investors were enthusiastic about it.

"Nihaal's out of the race?" A blond, blue-eyed Adonis asked softly as he took up residence on the couch. His legs stretched for miles in front of him and he handed Drake a beer bottle. "I was sent to give you this."

"Thank you." Drake took the longneck from the man. He grinned languidly. "Your Highness."

"Please," the Adonis invited smoothly. "Continue addressing me as Your Highness. It does wonders for my ego."

"You know what doesn't do wonders for your ego?" Shane asked cheerfully, carrying a monster bowl of organic sunflower seed chips. "Throwing up seven wonders in a row during basic training." He winked broadly at the blond Adonis. "Isn't that right, bud?"

Shane wasn't in his customary black bodyguard outfit, opting for jeans and an open plaid shirt over a black and red Menzo tee. In fact, he looked like a dark-haired twin of His Highness Alexander Heinrickson, because the prince of Stellangård also wore jeans, a plaid shirt and a Menzo tee.

After all, his family – the royal crown of Stellangård - owned a thirty percent stake in the racing team, same as Drake.

Alexander took a handful of chips and elegantly smushed them in his mouth opting to answer Shane's quip with finger action. A dull golden wedding band glinted on his left hand.

"If you two are done bickering, can we please settle down and watch the damn race?" Drake shot them both a fulminating glance.

They grinned at each other then threw a chip at him. He didn't have soldier-fast reflexes and so the missiles would have hit him square in the chest.

Luckily, they were intercepted by Bonzo, the world's largest terrier with an insatiable appetite. Bonzo's pink tongue swallowed the chips and he chewed them down in a second. Then, the dog draped itself over Drake and panted happily right in his face while Shane and Alexander watched his face contort from the weight of the dog and his tender ministrations.

"They have the food, you big lug." Drake tried to keep his beer out of the dog's reach. Bonzo's golden tail wagged and wagged, brushing against Drake's Armani casual twill trousers. "Go eat their face up."

"He loves you, Drake. You don't visit him nearly often enough," Swati said softly as she came into the living room carrying a loaded food tray. The palavers were closed but the aromas were enough to make Drake's stomach growl. In competition with the dog's panting whines.

Drake hauled Bonzo up by holding his hefty middle and plopping him on the floor. He quickly loped toward his mother-in-law and took the tray from her. "Let me take that from you, mama Swati."

Swati's lined face was instantly wreathed in smiles. She ran a hand over his arm, the only part of him she could reach. "Such a good beta you are, Drake. Almost as good as my Bonzo." She patted her knee and the dog rushed over to Swati, almost knocking Drake and his burden.

Bonzo gazed longingly at Drake from the safe cradle of his hooman's arms.

Drake shook his head, turned on his heel and went back to the TV station. Shane was sitting on his wing chair and Alexander innocently drank his beer, his mouth full of chips.

Drake set the tray of food down on the oak coffee table he'd had shipped from the Sumatran islands for Swati's birthday last year and glared at the both of them. "Are we in middle-school? You're in my spot. Get off."

Shane shrugged. "You vacated your spot for food. Even you can't have everything, one-percenter."

Alexander coughed and drank more of his beer lest he be drawn into the conversation.

Drake gave him a disgusted look which he did not return, preferring to fiddle with the label of the beer. "Traitor," he muttered at last and sat next to Alexander on the couch.

"That would be traitor, Your Highness," Alexander said snootily. He handed the chip bowl to Drake as a peace offering. "Manners maketh man, Fallahil."

Drake shook his head and munched on the chips. There was no point in lowering himself to Xander's level. The man was a former Marine, he did not have a problem getting down and dirty. "I thought, marriage would refine you. If not being the spare heir of a European principality."

Alexander shrugged. "Sasha likes my rough edges." He pushed his shoulder-length hair back in a soft gesture. "So I kept them. And I'm just the spare heir, thank god." He shuddered. "I'll leave the actual heir-ing to Michael."

Drake thought about Prince Michael and his gorgeous, intrepid wife Princess Daria, who were actually attending the grand prix, so the owners were represented. In fact, wouldn't you know it? Right then, the TV screen showed Prince Michael and Princess Daria as the cameras panned to them. They were tall, statuesque…royal. As they sat in the baking sun of a grand prix in the open stands.

Mili sat next to them, a huge hat shading her face from the brutal sun. She too wore a Menzo shirt. She waved excitedly at the camera while Michael and Daria, ever the golden, royal couple, stared straight ahead. Daria leaned in and whispered something to Michael and he looked gravely at her in return, but the camera panned to their hands, tightly clutched in each other's.

"The actual heir-ing includes indulging in PDA?" Drake asked idly.

"Why not?" Shane challenged. "What's wrong with indulging in PDA? Don't they deserve to be fully themselves everywhere?"

Drake grinned. He knew how to get Shane's goat, mention royal life and the man wound tighter than a coiled wire. It was so easy, it was almost no fun anymore. Almost. "I didn't say that, did I?"

Shane shot him the finger and settled even more comfortably in his wing chair, diverting his attention back to the screen.

Drake munched on more chips and contemplated the many wonderful vagaries of life. His, Shane's, Xander's. If someone had told him five years ago, he'd be beer buddies with some of the most powerful men on the planet – while saving the damn thing from its own worst impulses he'd have laughed in their faces. Sure, they were high.

After all, Drake Fallahil didn't do beer or friends. He didn't do saving the world. Not really. After all, these were such normal things, such small ordinary things that the having of them would have seemed beyond his reach. Because, he reached for the impossible, the extraordinary.

Things like creating The Verdant Fund, the world's multi-national geopolitical tech startup fund, focused slowly on initiatives – economic, financial, infrastructural *and* political – designed to make the world a cleaner, greener, better place to live in for future generations to come. Now, in its third year of institution, the four trillion global fund was slowly beginning to chip away and undo the decades of damage unchecked corporate governance had wreaked on world economies.

With the help of his friends, the Heinricksons and *their* friends who ran The Adya Foundation – a global charity dedicated to almost the same cause as The Fund – and the governments of seventeen nations, Verdant had established itself as a problem-solver, an excellent option for startup founders from all walks of life who had an idea that would reduce the burden of resource usage on earth.

In fact, this precise reason had brought together the triumvirate of Adya, the Heinricksons, and Drake to invest millions in Menzo Mondadnock's carbon-neutral engine being raced by Nihaal Bhatnagar, also one of the principal engineers on the project. No wonder, they all had a vested stake in the race today.

He'd done all this and more, Drake realized with a small smile of wonder, as a deep sense of contentment filled him. He'd done all this despite fully believing he couldn't. He didn't have it in himself to be the man everyone believed him to be. A hero.

What did he know of heroism?

He gazed at Shane and Xander trading stats on the different teams and discussing the probability of the race turning in their favor by lap thirty when the hard tires were changed for the softer ones. Xander and Shane were both former Marines, they'd seen real combat, real shit. And, given what Stellangård had been through for Michael to come to power, hero didn't even come close to describing their valor.

"What do you think, Drake?" Alexander enquired. "Did we nail it or what? You're the one who visited the pit yesterday to check out the new Baby." He sounded slightly peeved but also as if he was genuinely interested in Drake's opinion. Like it mattered.

Drake smiled broadly. "I was there by special invitation. Suckers. And yeah, lap thirty is when the engine starts cooling off because the tire pressure changes and New Baby really comes into her power. Now, if Nihaal can hold onto third position till then, we might get a chance at the podium."

"Awesome. I'll win the bet then." Shane pumped his fist in the air.

"What bet?" Xander asked, with interest.

Before Shane could answer, the narrow hallway in Swati's apartment in Little India filled with the shrieks of excited children and adults. Three of the little ones careened into the room followed by a tail-wagging Bonzo, yipping in excited barks. Kids and dog tumbled all over each other so more shrieks ensued.

Shane and Alexander looked at Drake and spoke in unison. "Not it."

Drake stood up and shook his head. "I cannot believe you two are scared of three children and a dog."

He ambled over to the middle of the room and tried to separate the tangle of arms, legs and furry paws. He only partially succeeded, because the dog transferred his attentions onto Drake and the kids grabbed onto his shoulders, chattering excitedly.

"Bharat," Drake hollered over the din. "Get your army under control." He shot Alexander a desperate look while the other man smirked. "Help, *please*."

Alexander stood up, walking with purpose toward the melee.

He whistled. Shrilly. The dog immediately rolled over on his belly and the kids froze.

For a moment, there was blessed calm in the room. Then three more kids burst into the room, followed by Bharat Shrinivasan's six-four form, hidden under a mountain of packages. He had a slightly hunted look on his cut face.

"Shane. Help!" He barked.

All the kids – varying in ages from three to six – swarmed over each other, the dog, Drake and Alexander who was caught in the middle.

Shane immediately relieved Bharat of a few packages.

Drake was pushed to his back by one of his nephews, Ahaan, a gap-toothed toddler who had his mother Sophia's infectious smile and was Bharat's son in weight.

"Tickle-wickle, Unkie Drake," he announced as he ran his pudgy, baby hands over Drake's chest.

"Stop, stop. The tickle monster has come!" Drake laughed breathlessly as the little boy continued to tickle him.

Alexander laughed even as he tried to corral the dog and two kids – Bharat's five-year-old Kushal and his own daughter Alexis – so they wouldn't kiss the dog to death. "Kids, please. Behave," he said feebly. "Lexy, baby. Why can't you be more like your cousin?"

Lexy's cousin, a tiny red-haired toddler crawled by with a sharp object in his teeth. Shane groaned and scooped the baby up one-handed while also maintaining control over the packages. "Meggie, how many times do we have to have this conversation? No. Chewing. Floor. Stuff."

The baby cooed and flapped her hands around and gazed adoringly at Shane with eyes so blue they were almost purple. "Your mom's going to win the damn bet," he muttered. "She *told* me I can't do a solo trip with you. She bet me I couldn't."

Drake's lips twitched at the helpless wonder in Shane. It was fun to see the man so undone.

"Oh, hush you, Shane." Swati bopped Shane's head and took the baby from him. "Don't you dare scold my precious little princess! Yes, yes." She beamed at the tiny baby in her hands. "You're my precious little princess."

"Kids!" A tiny, dark-haired general in a blue summer dress marched into the room. "What did I tell you about making noise while the dads are watching the race?"

She had her hands on her waist and glared at all the children on the floor. The dog subsided into whines.

"Sowie, mama," Ahaan wailed, holding his hands up so his mother could lift him. "Mama, liff. Liff."

Drake sat up, holding onto Ahaan, instantly jiggling him, then stood up in a fluid movement. He handed off the child to Sophia who mouthed a silent sorry to him. He gave her an 'it's okay' smile.

Kushal and Nehal, Bharat's twins were strangely quiet. Swati had a handle on Shane's Meggie while Alexander's Lexy and her little brother Ragnar (called Aggie) sat with their thumbs up in their mouths, on their daddy's lap.

For a second, only the sound of engines racing by at ungodly speeds could be heard. Even the two little ones stopped making sounds.

Bharat sighed. Loudly. "Is this what peace sounds like?"

Sophia glared at her husband. "Did you *have* to talk right then, Bharat?"

He held his hands up, packages and all, a glint of mutiny in his black eyes.

Shane, wise man that he was, stuck a chip in Bharat's mouth so he wouldn't say anything to offend his wife. He smiled silkily at Sophia and said, "There. Problem solved. Now we can enjoy the game in peace, yes?"

Under Sophia's stern eye – and she did have a rather terrifying stare perfected over raising three kids, two of whom were twins – the older kids settled on the floor in a neat line, with individual bowls of healthy chips and juices. They didn't even jostle each other for prime position next to Bonzo, who drooled in the middle while shooting side looks to Drake.

Swati held Meggie and rocked her, singing a traditional lullaby in her native tongue, Kannada. Ahaan settled with his mom while Alexander's Lexy chose to sit with her papa, cuddling close to him rather than hang out with her cousins and friends.

Drake gave an amused, indulgent smile as Xander listened attentively to Lexy's chatter, nodding here and there as if he totally understood and agreed with her jabbering.

Bharat took a sip of his cool beer and groaned, next to Drake on the couch. "Dude. You all ditched me, didn't you? There was no work emergency."

Drake grinned. "Nope. We just didn't want to spend the morning shopping and herding six kids and two women hopped up on sugar and credit cards."

Bharat gave him the evil eye. "One of these days, I'm going to get you back. You can't be so freaking smart all the time. It's unfair."

"I'm not the smart one, man," Drake protested. "I didn't invent a software that basically changed the way business is done forevermore."

"Nope," Sophia agreed. "That's my man, right there."

The smile she gave Bharat was positively smoldering, enough to make Drake clear his throat. Bharat nudged Drake and muttered, "We should do public spats more often. Then, Sophia can defend me. It's hot when she defends me."

"You're hopeless." Drake shook his head.

"You're jealous," Bharat shot back. "That there's no one to defend you."

"Who said so?" Anya Fallahil demanded as she swept into the room with all the flair of a queen. "Which black-hearted brigand dared make this accusation?"

"Not me." Bharat straightened from his slouch and gave his friend a slightly panicked look.

Xander and Shane immediately looked elsewhere while Drake enjoyed the fun.

Drake tried to keep the smile from taking over his face even as it took over his heart, instantly and completely. His wife wore a red summer dress that flirted with the knees of her spectacular legs and her curls flew around as she knelt and cuddled the dog and the kids, one by one. She squeezed her mother's hand and they discussed the food situation in undertones.

Then she stood up and advanced upon Shane in the wing chair. "You're in my spot," she announced.

"I was just watching the race," Shane protested.

"And so you can," Anya smiled sweetly. "From there." She pointed at the couch.

Shane gave Drake a dark look which he returned with innocence. Shane made Bharat scooch and squeezed into the three-seater with him and Drake.

Anya finally trained her golden gaze on her husband. She crooked one finger at him. The one with a giant sapphire ring, except it wasn't really sapphire. No, Anya had made Drake create a new metal artificially that would not be a burden on the earth and she wore it with pride every single day since they'd renewed their vows on a magical boat ride in Venice.

"Husband."

"Yes, wife?" Drake responded gravely.

"Why aren't you in your spot?"

Drake made a great show of dusting off crumbs from his hands. Then, taking his beer along with him, he dropped onto the wing chair.

Anya promptly dropped onto his lap, curling her arms around his neck. "Miss me?" She feathered the grey hair sprouting at the bottom.

"Yes," he answered with no hesitation.

The wicked glint in Anya's eyes softened, turned into golden lights of love and adoration. "I absolutely love how therapy has turned you into a communicator."

Drake squeezed Anya's bare ankle since her dress billowed around his lap. "I learned to communicate my needs really well."

She flexed against him. "That you never had a problem with, Fallahil."

Then she looked past him to the row of kids eating their snack and watching the race. "Just think," she murmured for his ears alone. "In seven months, we're going to have one of those for us."

Drake nodded. He felt giddy, panicked, insanely anxious and ferociously protective of the life growing inside Anya. The life he and she had made together, consciously. Choosing each other each step of the way. Through all that life had thrown at them.

"Good," he murmured. "Jake's a lonely child. He needs a little sister to play with."

Jake Fallahil was currently visiting Sentosa Island with his Lily aunt and Kit uncle, since he basically worshipped his older cousin brother Bret. High school senior Bret was Jake's favorite and only babysitter.

Having Jake had been the single-most terrifying decision in Drake's life. Especially because Anya had to go on bed rest for the last two months of her pregnancy.

"You're worried," Anya murmured, squeezing his neck in reassurance. "What are you worried about?"

He shook his head. "Nothing. Just…stuff." He didn't know how to articulate the idea of being a parent a second time when Anya marveled at his parenting skills with Jake. Jake was a smart, solemn boy with his mother's temper and his father's penchant for cards. A scary combination, truth be told. But one he'd made, with love and hope and all the wonder he possessed now because of the woman in his arms.

"You'll tell me later?" Anya turned around and yelled at the screen. "Overtake him at the chicane, Nihaal! Come on, man!"

"I will," Drake answered. "I promise."

Anya looked around the room. Drake followed her gaze. Everyone was occupied with the race or a child or, in Bharat and Sophia's case, making googly eyes at each other. Then she covered his mouth with hers, cupping his jaw and giving him a bit of tongue.

When she broke the kiss he gave her a mind-whacked look. "What was that for?"

"That was for you. Being you. Being mine," she answered cheekily.

Then she settled her head on his shoulder and they looked at the screen, where the thirtieth lap was coming up, finally. "We're going to win, aren't we?" she asked softly.

Drake looked around the room, full of his family – newfound and chosen and inherited. Then at the woman in his arms – the blood in his heart, the vision he always tried to live up tp. Then, at the race on the screen, which was costing him upwards of twenty five million. The least important thing in his life.

And he answered the only way he could, "We already have, sweetheart. We already have."

~ ~ ~ ~ ~

Want more Ruthless Billionaires? Then **get the next book** right now. Where Drake's fiery and feisty assistant finally meets her match in a playboy F1 champion who is hiding demons of his own.

BURN

Ruthless Billionaires Book 2

Twenty years ago, a very wealthy Italian named Ricardo Braggatti had wanted a Ferrari Kenzo, and had had to wait three months for it to be shipped to Palermo, where he lived in wealthy seclusion, in a humongous villa. He'd decided that building the sports machine was better than waiting ninety whole days.

What emerged was the very first machine that rolled under the name of Menzo Monadnock, a blatant insult to the Ferrari Kenzo. He liked his own car so much; he decided to mass produce it. The name Menzo had since then been associated with some very fine pieces of sports cars. And pleasure cars.

They were slowly gaining a foothold, when his son, Antonio, had the very bright idea of launching a racing team on the racing circuit, for the company to gain worldwide recognition and fame. They had entered with the Indy circuit and even tried NASCAR for a year or two, all the while applying for patents for an original chassis.

Their engineers had finally come through and Luke Braggatti, Ricardo's grandson, headed the F1 racing team, which came into the game seven years ago. Their first pair of drivers were relative biggies who left them, when they failed to place with the cars provided.

The engines were replaced, and so was the manager. Paul Lacroix entered the picture and he brought with him two outstanding mechanics. Gerhard Winderhorn, a lumbering German who was a genius with a carburetor and such like, and Nihaal Bhatnagar, a taciturn Indian who turned out to be a genius at the steering wheel.

Two months after Lacroix was hired, he ran Nihaal for the first time, in the family's annual Fiesta F1, where all the corporate bigwigs competed for the Golden Urn.

Nihaal drove a Corvette. And he was still faster than his closest rival, Luke himself, by three point three seconds.

Two weeks later, Nihaal replaced their first wheel driver at the F1 circuit. He won his first race at Magny-Cours three weeks later.

He had not looked back since. Neither had Menzo Monadnock.

This year would be the crowning glory for Menzo because they were in contention for the Construction Championship and because Nihaal was in the top three positions for The Driver's Championship.

He had placed of the last fourteen races, and come second in the other four. The only two ahead of him were Hamilton of Ferrari, and Verstappen, also of Ferrari.

They each had two points more than him. And Max was not racing today, the last race, because he had suffered a leg sprain during Practise on Friday. Menzo and the entire crowd wanted a Menzo and Nihaal win.

So did Nihaal.

It was twenty minutes to race time.

~ ~ ~ ~ ~ ~

Nihaal hit the showers along with the other drivers. All of them were a superstitious lot, and were doing all the routine things they did before a race. His racing partner, a blond British Adonis named Tom Lutherton, was singing a song from the movie Grease.

All around them, they could hear a cacophony of voices and noises. Some were singing. Others were cursing. Some were even praying.

Nihaal was silent as he stood under the steady shower of the spray, and let the water run off him. The pressure was kept at maximum so that it would hit all of the vital points and leave him loose and limber for the three hours ahead.

He emerged, seven seconds later and, unconcerned with so much nudity, toweled off, wrapping it around his lean hips, walked towards his locker. His partner, Tom was already getting into his suit.

"Hit it, already, old man. Or, you'll be late, and I'll take your pole." Tom grinned as he slicked the wet from his hair and banged his locker. He kept the photo of his wife, Gracie, six months pregnant, near his heart. Tom was one of the few devoted racers who was also a devoted husband.

It was amusing to watch him play stud during race weekend, when everyone knew he would always run to back to his pretty blonde wife the minute the race was over. It was amusing and sweet, and Nihaal thought so.

His mind was calm, his thoughts centered, as he didn't bother to reply to his partner's remarks.

He wanted nothing to detract from this moment. From this day.

From this race.

Nihaal Bhatnagar was going out for the race of his lifetime, and he was going out to win.

~ ~ ~ ~ ~

After the race

There was only one way to describe him. *Fucking naked.*

Mili's heart pounded a jungle drum in her ears while she stared at the expanse of outrageously toned, exquisitely perfect, mouthwatering flanks of Formula One racing's golden boy. His thighs were sculpted things of hard marble sewn with honey brown skin that flexed each time the water hit his striated back. And his buttocks were perfect moons of hardness and flesh. *Delicious.*

He was whistling tunelessly as he showered in the glass cubicle of the hotel bathroom, the door carelessly flung open. So anyone, *her,* could wander inside and get an arresting eyeful.

Don't look down, Mili.

Mili looked down. Spit dried in her throat when she saw the outrageously, perfectly beautiful specimen between his legs. And had the most explicit vision of what it would be like if she went inside right now, got down on her knees and took it in her mouth, the warm water of the shower cascading around them both.

Wet warmth rushed between her legs. Tightening the skin under the loose pants and lacy shell cinched at the waist y a handtooled faux leather belt. Slicking her core against the silk of her Cosabella thongs, while her nipples peaked against the matching silk of her bra.

She drew another sharp breath. As excitement and anger filled her veins.

What the fuck was she thinking? Mili Iyer did not kneel for anyone. Certainly not a man. Not even a man as sexy and perfectly built as this one.

She shook her head once. Took a deep breath to calm her pulsing heart and to bring forth the legendary cool she was known for, globally. The cool she'd won by being assistant to Drake Fallahil, a man who'd made his billions with nothing more than his sharp wit and his sharper brain. She'd assisted him in building his empire while studying for her undergraduate and graduate degrees *and* law, later on.

So a naked man should not derail her determination or her equilibrium.

Then again, she wasn't determined or calibrated equally. Not anymore. Not since the last year.

So, here she was. Flustered and aroused and *aware* of this man singing horribly in his bathroom. While she skulked outside it like some lovestruck groupie. God, she was pathetic.

And it wouldn't do. She'd come here for a job. She needed to do it. Then get the hell out before her head exploded with lust or something far worse. *Shame.* At being caught in such a humiliating position.

Unfortunately, for Mili, fate stepped in like the bitch she was.

Mili took a step forward just as Nihaal Bhatnagar turned in the shower.

Heat rushed through her, suffusing her being. Just as the wet had filled her insides moments ago.

Nihaal's beautifully chiseled face froze in mid-tune. His Adam's apple bobbed up and down but no sound came out. Water poured down his truly athletic physique, delineating each set of muscle and bones.

"I'm sorry," Mili said politely. "For barging in."

To his immense credit, the racer did nothing more than nod at her. He did not cover himself or look enraged at this gross invasion of his privacy. He just stood there, with water falling on him. A god in his prime.

"Why?" Nihaal asked.

Like silk. Like dark desires and whispered promises best broken. His voice, the cadence and accent of it, was more tempting than his body.

"Because I'm here to deliver extremely awful news, Mr. Bhatnagar."

Nihaal cocked his head.

The width of the room stood between them. A healthy hundred feet. But she felt the force of his dark eyes directly on her face. On her very skin. As if a freaking spotlight had landed on her, magnifying her for him alone.

"Yes?"

"I'm sorry," she said again, in a voice rusty with discomfort. "Your father's dead."

"I beg your pardon?" Nihaal asked coolly. But he was naked and there was no way to hide the clench of his fists and the tautening of his stance. "What did you just say?"

His defensiveness erased her discomfort. Made her bolder. Stand up taller. Gave heft and gravity to her words. "Your father, Krishna Bhatnagar, owner of Bhatnagar

Champion and Stud Farm, is dead." And then, because it was best to deliver all the bad news at once, she plunged on. "You'll have to come home. To The Homestead. In Kolkata. To take care of his last rites since you're his son and heir."

Then, Nihaal did the least expected thing of all.

He looked her straight in the eye. And laughed.

Mili knew, right then, that her mission had turned from difficult to impossible. And there was nothing she could do about it.

ACKNOWLEDGMENTS

I'd like to thank quite a few people who made the writing of this book possible --

Priyanka Menon, who screwed my head on straight with the vax scene. Thanks, love. I adore you so much.

Bri Blackwood and Ivy Mason, two fantastic billionaire dark romance authors who held my hand and helped instil a new level of confidence in me. Thank you, fabulous ladies.

My incredible team, my family and friends, without whom I'm simply lost sometimes.

And lastly, Aarti's Awesome ARCsters, bookstagrammers, and every single reader friend. Your love and support buoys me, keeps me going, and makes all the aches and pains worth it. I'm so lucky to have you so I can do this, all day every day.

The show Ishq Par Zor Nahin. My mom's obsessed with this series and so I wrote the heroine, Ishqi, of the show into Drake and Anya's story! Hope you like this birthday gift, mama.

ABOUT THE AUTHOR

Hi, there I'm Aarti V Raman. I write all shades and forms of romance or will in the future because I suffer from writing attention deficit disorder. I must tell all the stories! So, my romances range from romantic comedy, chick lit to romantic suspense and dark romance starring tortured billionaires and suffering military types!

Before I turned to writing and telling these stories full-time, I was a teacher, business journalist and editor for close to fifteen years. So my heroines are career-minded, city-living, strong-willed hot messes who still have their lives together. I believe in writing what I know and I know me best so most of these heroines are Indian (South Asian women of color).

I also believe in writing more of what I want so my heroes are indecently hot, filthy rich, fiendishly smart with secret hearts of gold. Thus, the angst and steam-meter are off the charts when stubborn force meets immovable object on the way to happy ever after. So does the banter and danger, because what's love without a little bit of jeopardy, am I right?

I'm a TEDx speaker and 22 of my romances have hit the Amazon Bestseller Charts so I can proudly call myself an Amazon 100 International Bestselling Author. My chick lit dramedy "The Worst Daughter Ever" has been optioned for screen. My bestselling Millionaire Foes series is part of the Writers on the Moon Project, on a time capsule to go to the actual moon.

I'm also known as Writer Gal. I live in Mumbai with my large and largely loveable extended family in a version of my three favorite words – Happy Ever After.